TANGLING WITH THE LONDON TYCOON

A BRICK SQUARE NOVEL

TANGLING WITH THE LONDON TYCOON

A BRICK SQUARE NOVEL

SUZI JENNINGS

Entangled Publishing, LLC
2614 South Timberline Road
Suite 109
Fort Collins, CO 80525
Visit our website at www.entangledpublishing.com.

Indulgence is an imprint of Entangled Publishing, LLC.

Edited by Wendy Chen
Cover design by Erin Dameron-Hill
Cover art from iStock

Manufactured in the United States of America

First Edition February 2017

Chapter One

Rosco Redmond was an opportunity Kitty couldn't afford to mess up.

The door to his Georgian town house lacked any attempt at welcome. It faced the world with immaculate London style—glossy black paint against warm cream stone—handsome but unadorned.

The peaceful, exclusive inner city cobblestone street oozed understated elegance. Its sweep of heritage buildings an oasis of secluded tranquility, just a few blocks away from London's hectic commercial center.

But it had Kitty's heartbeat thundering in her ears as unwanted memories flooded her in a cold tide of rejection. Memories of the miserable childhood she'd purged from her adult life.

It was the worst coincidence that the Redmond house looked an awful lot like her childhood home and represented the kind of world Kitty never wanted to be part of again.

The unexpected shock had all her buried insecurities nibbling at her confidence.

But she'd never walked away from a challenge since she was sixteen, when her mother died and left her alone. A time of shame, of dark and painful memories usually left undisturbed and firmly in the past where they belonged.

Shaking them off now, she faced the house squarely, rocking discreetly from foot to foot to ease the ache of her highest heeled boots. She'd chosen them for courage, so she didn't mind the pain.

Straightening her back, she commanded her nerves to focus and smiled as her fingers caressed the worn strap of the camera hung around her neck.

She could do this job.

Plucked at short notice from the lowest ranks of LJ Redmond Publishing's contracted photographers for this urgent assignment, she couldn't believe her luck. It was a matter of timing, the human resources department had informed her, because all of Mr. Redmond's senior photographers were unavailable at this time.

She would do whatever was required, as her financial security depended on nailing this project—whatever it turned out to be—and taking her best photos ever.

Kitty took one last look at the imposing three-story building, sucked in a deep breath, and bounded up the four steps to the porch. She found the discreetly recessed doorbell and pressed it for a long, determined ring.

Hoisting her camera bag onto her hip, she took another steadying breath as the sound of security locks opening reminded her this was serious business.

Then Rosco Redmond, CEO of his family's Investment and Publishing Groups, stood in the doorway. She'd expected a butler in coattails or a housekeeper to answer the door.

The man himself was tall, lean, and gorgeous. Tailored for business in an impeccable dark suit and blood-red tie.

Untouchable reserve emanated from him, as if stitched

into every precise seam of his clothing. As hard-edged and private as the stone facade of his home.

And he was sexy.

She wasn't prepared for sexy. Certainly not based on the one formal portrait she'd been able to find on the company's website.

For a big city, old money tycoon whose name was always in the financial news, her hasty internet search had revealed surprisingly few photos of him. No grainy early morning snaps of him stumbling out of night clubs or tuxedoed celebrity event poses to boost a philanthropic profile. And zilch tabloid love matches.

"I'm Kitty Mayfair," she said, finding her voice and infusing it with a firmness aimed to match the sternness of the face looking down at her.

"You're late." His voice, deep and brisk with an unexpected Irish burr, had her toes curling uncontrollably inside her boots, all pain forgotten.

"Only by ten minutes. Peak hour travel takes time," she shot back as his hardened blue eyes assessed her.

The urge to tug on the hem of her suddenly-too-short knitted coat fought with the need to appear totally assured.

In addition to those favorite confidence-boosting boots, she'd pulled on comfortable winter leggings and anchored her layers of woolens with an oversized leather belt and a raspberry beret, all of which failed to scream professional.

Why hadn't she taken five minutes to borrow a corporate-smart suit from her sister? She suppressed a sigh. Typical.

He grimaced, looking down at her as if she was an untidily wrapped, unwanted parcel planted on his doorstep. "Travel time needs to be pre-planned for an inner city assignment."

"Look," she said, when she really meant *stop looking and take me seriously*, "your personal assistant gave me two hours' notice for this meeting. I needed to postpone a client and travel halfway across London."

He nodded, his disapproval cool and courteous, but despite his continued glare, she sensed innate good manners. A code of conduct she hoped she could use to her advantage.

She placed one foot on his doorstep and rested the weight of the camera bag on her thigh. "I've prepared as thoroughly as time allowed and packed all the equipment I thought I might need, given that you haven't provided any assignment details."

He nodded again, still not speaking, and she stared back at him, trying to gauge both his mood and her confused reaction to him.

"Hair," Kitty heard herself squeak before she could stop it. She cleared her suddenly parched throat. "You have hair." She couldn't rein in her accusatory tone. "You're bald on your website." He was supposed to be bald. Bald, paunchy, pipe-smoking, maybe.

Not sexy.

He frowned and, almost absent-mindedly, brushed his hand through his thick dark waves. "A close shave for a favorite charity. Very cold in winter. Not to be repeated."

Interesting. A one-off look, yet the one he chose to represent his business. And some dry humor hidden behind his unsmiling demeanor. But before she could process that contradictory mix—bald but not, formidable but willing to "let his hair down" for charity—he parried back with a personal barb of his own.

"You're not the person I was expecting. You're much too young. Show me your identification."

She bit down on a rude reply and fumbled in her bag for ID. *Don't get defensive*, she warned herself as she felt her temper flare. *It's his employer's right to check out his employees.*

She held his gaze as she flashed her photo ID. The importance of getting into this man's house and taking her best photos ever fired up her resolve again.

Kitty needed this assignment to develop her studio. And to cement her financial contribution to the business complex she was developing with her four half sisters. Sisters she hadn't known existed until just eighteen months ago.

Plus, she had a dream photography proposal of her own to submit to LJ Redmond Publishing, and this sudden elevation up the ranks to actually meet the CEO himself made that a possibility.

No, she hadn't scrambled to keep this appointment to be left on the doorstep.

Rosco quirked a challenging eyebrow at her, and Kitty lifted her chin and narrowed her eyes right back at him, ready to fight for this opportunity.

He might be the country's most successful publisher of the high-end photography books everyone wanted on their coffee table, but he wasn't going to put her off that easily.

"Young? Not very..." she said, aiming for breezy but mature with a touch of irony. "I'm cursed with a twenty-nine-year-old baby face and an untimely taste for mashed vegetables."

There was no answering acknowledgement of humor. "But I know how to use a camera." His gaze still didn't soften. "Expertly."

An odd feeling of silent impasse settled between them and prickled along her own hairline.

She remained braced. Every muscle tensed to continue the fight. Every hormone called to order as they vibrated in an unwanted response to his warrior pose—a man in command of his territory.

A sudden commotion on the street made them both jump, and Kitty turned her head to see what the noise was. But she wouldn't take her foot off the doorstep and risk losing her advantage.

Two scooters had clattered over the cobbles and screeched to a halt, their front wheels mounting the shallow first porch step.

Cameras clicked. Male voices called from faces hidden behind black helmet visors. "Titania. Rosco. Look this way. Beauty and money, Rosco. Mixing business and pleasure, eh mate?"

Kitty ducked her head in horror. Paparazzi. The last thing she wanted was to be aligned to that brand of photography.

Rosco growled in Kitty's ear and snagged his arm around her shoulders, spinning her toward him. Her nose grazed the soft silk of his tie as she steadied herself against his chest.

"Inside. Now," he ordered, his contemptuous tone a whisper. His breath was warm against the top of her head.

A hint of sharp citrus cologne cut through her senses as her nose remained buried against him, and she wriggled to put some breathing space between them. She needed air.

Pulling back a fraction, her chin grazed his chest as she raised her eyes to his. Hot anger glittered back at her before thick black lashes shut her out.

But it was too late to protect her from the burn. The heat of his anger froze her in his embrace. She was in danger. Past and present trapping her in a public nightmare that made no sense.

"You've got some explaining to do," she told his tie, its precision knot tight at his throat, its dark red color perfectly matching her mood.

Dimly, she heard more shouts. "Titania. Look this way. Rosco. What's the duke going to say about this?"

Rosco growled again and pulled her into the house, her heels skittering on the marble floor as he slammed the door shut.

She clutched at his arm for balance, breathing a little heavier. She steeled herself against both his grim, angry glare and another flutter low in her stomach.

His muscles clenched taut and strong beneath her fingers. The fine wool of his suit jacket an expensive symbol of business success and power.

He steadied her quickly and moved away.

"What was that all about?" she said, anger and nerves making her jittery. "Who is Titania?" she asked, annoyed at the slight wobble in her voice. This was a drama she could do without.

"You really don't know?"

His tone was hard and uncomfortably close to disbelief. "No, I really don't know anything about any of this." She worked to keep her voice steady and professional.

"We'll see if that's the truth," he said through gritted teeth as they heard the scooters roar off with a cheeky blast of their horns. "Titania is my celebrity event–organizing sister's famous client and bridesmaid."

"The pop star? *That* Titania is your sister's bridesmaid?"

"Yes."

"Am I here for a celebrity shoot?"

"Absolutely not."

"That would have been a surprise. There's nothing like that in my portfolio. But Titania is hot right now."

"Too hot for me," he said with an edge of disgust. "And nothing to do with me. Whatever the papers want to invent."

"I'm with you there," she said, thinking fast and deciding to ignore his questioning her honesty. She knew she was telling the truth and she couldn't let this mayhem affect her contract. "I hate celebrity gossip."

"You arrived with the cameras," he said as he folded his arms across his chest and remained braced against the door, keeping the world out and her pinned in his sights.

"I. Did. Not." There was no wobble in her voice now. Hot indignation blazed through her. She might not look like a corporate professional, but tipping off the paparazzi was something she would never do. She had some personal appreciation of how awful media scrutiny could be, but she wasn't about to explain that to him.

"This is not my choice. They must have thought I was your Titania."

"I told you, she isn't *my* Titania."

"Just a mix-up then. I guess we're both tall with long dark hair." She'd appeal to his fairness, hoping he had some.

"Well, you certainly don't have her pop star glamour."

Kitty bristled. She had nothing to be ashamed of. He'd looked down on her since he'd opened the door, and his light Irish brogue didn't soften the words.

"You don't trowel on the makeup, I'll give you that," he continued, eyeing her face with obvious dislike. It was a backhanded compliment, but she grabbed it as a path back to the reason she was here.

"My profession is in the background. I don't want to be the center of attention, but I do want to do my best work." She hoisted her bag higher on her hip and turned away from him. "I didn't tip off the paparazzi," she said forcefully.

She was inside his house. And she wasn't leaving. Not without a contract. And certainly not to face another round with the paparazzi. Not without an explanation of why she had unknowingly been invited to walk into their ambush.

Stepping into the center of the foyer, she finally registered her surroundings. The warmth. The delicious aroma of home cooking. The spacious splendor of marble flooring and a sweeping staircase leading her eye up to a double-vaulted ceiling.

Memories swirled around her. Snapshots of her childhood. "It's just as I remember," she whispered, the sudden loneliness chilling her. Snapshots minus a father and crowded with her mother's wealthy "gentlemen friends."

"You've been here before?" Rosco's tone revealed how unlikely he thought that would be.

Kitty turned; she'd almost forgotten him for a second. "No." She ignored his tone with its edge of condescension. "I grew up in a house like this. Not far from here."

"Hmmm…" he said with a wealth of skeptical evaluation just under his breath.

Damn, this guy with his all-male control was getting to her.

She never dwelt on her childhood and—until today—she'd been able to avoid revisiting any reminders of her mother's world. Switching off the past had suddenly gotten harder.

"This way," he said, interrupting her memories. "We have just a few minutes to finalize our contract."

He led her into a gracious, comfortable living room. Floor-to-ceiling windows arched over a lush autumn garden, and a warm fire glowed beneath a solid marble mantle lined with family photos.

They neatly framed the differences between the Redmond world and hers. Images of family occasions hadn't added any weight to Kitty's rucksack in the eight years she'd traveled the world as a photographer.

Family commitment just wasn't in her DNA.

She turned her back on the pictures and perched on the edge of a plush cream chair, carefully placing her bag at her feet.

"You will be undertaking all photography for my sister's wedding this weekend," he said, getting straight to the point while gathering contract papers from a writing desk beside the fire.

Kitty let stunned silence fall between them. She'd never been a wedding photographer, had no albums in her portfolio or on her website.

And this probably wasn't the time to enlighten him about her views on marriage. She didn't do weddings. Happily-ever-afters in taffeta and tiaras didn't ring true for her.

"You will be recompensed for any work lost, and I'll expect you to be available starting today." He sat on the sofa opposite her. "Tomorrow, Friday, I will expect you at the wedding rehearsal. The wedding will take place on Saturday afternoon at a confidential rural location."

Questions raced across her mind, and she tried to sort them into two logical lists. Sensible to ask. Unwise to ask. The last thing she wanted to do was jeopardize this contract.

"Why am I here if you think I look too young for the job?" she blurted out before any list making was completed. His words still prickled her pride.

He sighed and ran his hand through his hair. "I thought you were older. Fifty-something. Your personnel file obviously has an incorrect date of birth. An unacceptable mistake made by my HR department." He angled another critical glance at her and then quickly looked away.

"So the paparazzi confusing me with Titania was as shocking to you as it was to me?"

"Quite." He cleared his throat.

"Your photography style is real and totally lacking in glitz. That's what I want for my sister's wedding album. I'll be supervising you closely and advising on all details."

Close supervision. Kitty opened her mouth to protest then shut it quickly as her common sense finally disciplined her thoughts.

She nodded, mustering polite professionalism. "Why such short notice, may I ask?"

"My sister's photographer fractured her collar bone."

"I'm sorry. That sounds painful," Kitty said, feeling some sympathy for the woman, even as her creative juices surged at her good luck.

"I consider it a fortunate accident," he continued with the merest nod of matching sympathy, totally at odds with his words. "Her glamorous style was not my choice."

He adjusted the cuff of the crisp white shirt beneath his suit and glanced at the gold Rolex on his wrist. "So are we in agreement? A few days of your time and my technical supervision?"

Not so fast, she thought. She'd deal with the supervision clause and his arrogant boardroom manner later, but the paparazzi was another level of complication she couldn't ignore.

"I'll need that contract to cover the possible media fallout from my arrival," she said, vulnerability gnawing at her confidence again. She worked to steady her nerves, unable to stop one clammy palm from smoothing her coat over her knees. "I want anonymity."

He shot her a sharp, skeptical look. "Is there something you're hiding from me?"

"I told you, I'm a professional." She returned his direct tone. "I don't want any association with tabloid journalism."

He continued to evaluate her, and she schooled her face to hide the turmoil she felt. Business only. The contract was nearly hers.

He grimaced, looking less than convinced, and Kitty held her breath.

"We'll proceed," he said with a curt nod. "I can't speak for rogue photographers, but between us, anonymity is agreed." He added a handwritten paragraph to the contract. "I certainly won't be releasing your name to the press, but the confidentiality implied will be mutual. I'll need ongoing assurance you are not working with the press."

He raised his eyes, a dark blue storm, back to hers. "Agreed?"

"Agreed," she said, returning the bite in his tone, unable

to tear her gaze from his. His insinuations were insulting, but more importantly, she needed to know more about the situation she found herself in.

"Who is the duke and why might I, in my Titania decoy guise, be of interest to him?" she asked, barely hiding her annoyance at the autocratic power he packaged so immaculately in his suited armor. "Pertinent to my anonymity, I think?"

His jawed clenched tight, and she felt her own molars grind as she waited.

Finally he spoke, with obvious reluctance and a cold glance of warning. "My company is competing for a photography contract recording the history of a private palace owned by the Duke of Sandford and his wife Trinity St. George. I believe this media rubbish is being driven by our competitor."

The only words she heard were "Trinity St. George." Surely there could be only one.

The name jittered along her nerves, back to bad memories and old dramas. Her late mother's on-again, off-again friend from all those years ago. An "it" girl who had played and won the trump card of ambitious models. Marriage into the aristocracy.

"Will they be at the wedding?" she asked, her voice sounding thin.

"No. I don't mix business with pleasure. You won't be involved."

Kitty nodded her understanding, no longer trusting her voice to conceal her anxiety. As long as they never met, Trinity St. George wasn't important. Kitty couldn't endure this Titania mix-up if it threw her into Trinity St. George's orbit and back into the spotlight of her late mother's life.

What mattered was the next few days. A wedding and quality photography. A challenge she could meet and use to impress Rosco Redmond.

She looked past him to the comforting flames of the fire and let them sooth her frayed nerves—she needed some control and clarification here.

"You hugged me. The cameras will freeze frame that." She willed her voice to be strong as she returned her attention to his face.

"I did not hug you," he said as she watched deep anger blaze again in his eyes. "I don't hug employees. I merely pulled you to safety, away from the cameras."

"So you accept I have no part in their ambush at your door?" She wouldn't let that fiction linger between them any longer.

He barely inclined his head, his face unreadable.

It wasn't good enough for her.

"Concern for my safety implies you accept I was also at risk. I don't have affairs with employers."

He gave her a hard stare, and she met it head on, anger stiffening her spine. "Surely you were also concerned about your own *safety*."

She had no problem loading the word "safety" with innuendo. He was the public figure under threat here. She was merely a bit player, a private person who had walked into his high-powered, complicated life.

"Yes." His tone was so curt it offered no hint of trust or information sharing. "The appearance of a hug between us was purely accidental, unavoidable in the circumstances."

Unavoidable? She wasn't convinced. How much had been reflexive self-preservation and how much had been employer intimidation?

His voice again dripped disdain. "The last thing my professional reputation needs is an implied alliance with Titania's youthful partying and late night clubbing. But the less you know the better," he said, and snapped his attention back to the contract in his hand.

So he thought he had more to lose than she did. She allowed herself a welcome break from the hard lines of his face and once again took comfort in the flicker of the fire.

For now, she was on the CEO's professional radar, and she wasn't letting the past, or the sexy haughtiness of the man himself, mess with that.

But it niggled her that he seemed as disdainful of her as he was of Titania. Almost as ashamed of being associated with her as he was with the pop star's public image.

Then the front door slammed, stopping her thoughts, and she was grateful to shrug them off as female laughter filled the foyer and another round of paparazzi shouting could be heard from the street.

"Time's up." Rosco jumped to his feet and thrust the contract toward her. "Sign it quickly."

She jerked her attention from the warmth of the flames and watched him stride out of the room with an urgency that had her flicking directly to the last page and adding her signature.

Whatever complications lie ahead, and her gut told her there would be plenty, they weren't going to derail her future. She now had a signed contract.

Chapter Two

Rosco swore under his breath and readied himself for arguments as he shepherded his two sisters, Amanda and Fiona, and his four-year-old niece, Cara, into the living room.

Home from yet another pre-wedding shopping trip, they jostled designer bags and coffees-to-go with ease, excited about the paparazzi scrum outside the house in a way that set his teeth on edge.

Their chatter stopped as Kitty rose to meet them, smoothing the short woolen creation she was wearing over her slim hips.

He found her unexpected youth an annoyingly attractive complication.

He was usually immune to her sort of colorful femininity, especially in the workplace where, years ago, his late father's history of dalliance had shattered his mother and blighted the company's professional reputation. But the shock of Kitty's long, long legs and thigh-high boots had taken him off guard. Hardly surprising, as he *was* expecting a middle-aged, comfortably shod, senior professional. He would kick HR's ass for their sloppy record-keeping.

Their error had forced him into the sort of public spotlight he hated. And his fumbled attempt to get Kitty inside and away from paparazzi was a monumental gaffe that had made matters worse. He'd had no intention of hugging her, but she was right. It would be framed to look like something it wasn't.

He abhorred any hint of coercion or threat to integrity, yet he'd acted without his usual caution. The assault on his privacy and the hint of horror he'd glimpsed on Kitty's face had knocked him off-balance.

She'd seemed vulnerable, her hair soft against his cheek, for the brief second she was nestled against his chest.

It was almost as if she had fit there. Just right.

He let go of that fanciful sentiment immediately. She'd argued her point and the contract details like a professional. Forget the feel of her against his body… She wasn't his type. And he never had personal feelings about employees.

He shook his head, marshalled his grip on business, and commanded the attention of his soon-to-be-married sister. "Amanda. Meet Kitty Mayfair, your new photographer." It was a done deal. He wasn't giving his sister any wiggle room.

"I told you, Titania is sorting someone from her PR team."

Damned if he'd allow any more attention-seeking Hollywood flashiness in what was quickly becoming a publicity fiasco.

"We don't have time for debate. Kitty is contracted through the company and available now," he said, completing the formal introductions to his family.

"In charge as usual, Rosco." Amanda's tone purred dangerously mild to his suspicious ears as she smiled warmly at Kitty.

"If her photos are as fabulous as her boots, we'll be instantly on the same page." She wrinkled her nose at him in obvious amusement.

Kitty smiled at Amanda and ignored him. She wasted no time whipping out a tablet from her bag and showing the women her website and portfolio.

Annoyance and foreboding crawled through him as his sisters and excited little niece clustered round her. He smelled trouble and the beginnings of a familiar female conspiracy.

Let them think they were in charge for now.

The restraint required to put up with never ending trivial details, all for the sake of giving his sister the wedding experience she wanted, was testing to say the least.

He'd known when he'd woken up that morning to find his niece sprinkling him with fairy dust that this was just the beginning of an excessively female few days.

He adored having Cara stay in the house. It didn't happen often enough. Apart from the worry of having to remember to wear pajamas, in case of sparkly wake-up calls, he couldn't think of a better reason to take a break from work.

In fact, Cara was about the only reason he would consider not working. And the fact there was another wedding saga about to begin.

He'd been through it all five years ago with Cara's mother, Fiona, when he'd had total control of the wedding planning.

Fiona shared his preference for privacy, and she'd been content to let him manage all the photography and low-key media exposure.

Their mother had been alive then, too, and had Amanda's exuberance under control.

Now his publicity-loving youngest sister had hurtled out of student jeans into corporate suits and bought a designer wedding dress he was forbidden to see. As an event agent to the stars, her taste for an occasion was bound to demand a dress way outside his own formal preferences.

She'd inherited their late father's "sociable" personality and would happily be all over social media and the celebrity pages.

The timing couldn't be worse.

His negotiations to win the contract for the pictorial history of the Duke of Sandford's private palace were nearing completion.

The duke, teetering on the brink of commitment, was known for his conservative social commentary and insistence on high journalistic standards.

The paparazzi were not an acceptable part of Rosco's strategy.

And neither, on a personal level, was the visitation of his aunts. Yet again he was just a few days away from a wedding and matchmaking hell. This time without the moderating influence of his mother.

The bridesmaid jokes, made ominously worse this time with the Titania connection.

The invitations to dance. He didn't do dancing. Especially at weddings with his aunts, Cupid's elderly cohorts, watching.

His mind was kept busy strategizing his way through the whole performance with as little human interaction as possible.

He was considering joining the washing-up staff, or developing a short but highly infectious illness.

Matrimonial man-flu.

Unfortunately, he was famed throughout the family for his excellent immune system.

If only this damn wedding was equally immune to drama.

For his family, he'd have to accept the fallout from this morning's photos of himself and Kitty Mayfair, as if caught in some way only a tabloid could hint at. At least his impromptu hug with Kitty gave him some control over the Titania rumors.

Any hint he was personally involved with the pop star would throw him into the type of spotlight he'd spent his entire adult life avoiding.

The type of spotlight his late father's reckless, alcohol-fueled sense of fun would have reveled in. Disregarding the financial and reputation consequences.

The instant rapport happening in front of him now did nothing to allay his fears. Amanda's and Kitty's shared laughter was raising the hairs on the back of his neck.

Time to break it up.

He scooped his niece up into a hug and she squealed with delight, as he knew she would. If only her look-a-like aunt was as cooperative.

He kissed Cara's blond curls and handed her to her mother. "Time for a nap while I organize a pre-wedding photography shoot."

Fiona grinned as she took her daughter from him. "Good luck with that, brother." She waggled her fingers at him. "Back soon for the battle score."

Rosco scowled after her as Amanda rounded on him. "I'll oversee the photography. I know what I want."

He pinched the bridge of his nose. "Amanda you *don't* know what you want." He threw his arms in the air, beseeching her and the silent, amused-looking Kitty to listen to him. "It's been white bows, then pink roses, then silver ribbons, then gold sequins, and that's just for the pew decorations."

"That's me thinking aloud." Amanda tossed her hair. "Go away, Rosco. It's my wedding."

"And it's my *responsibility.*" He ground out that last word, hoping his authority covered the exasperation and, surprisingly, the exhaustion he was feeling.

What a tidal wave of feminine frippery this week had been. And there was worse to come when Titania, and then his aunts, arrived. Two very different but equally galling threats to his peace of mind.

At least he could control the public perception. This was about family reputation, about his mother, her legacy, and the coup of a deal he was about to seal on her behalf with the duke and his wife.

He planted his hands on his hips and faced Amanda. "I will oversee all the photography. Evaluate technique and suitability of the photos." He wanted formal, serious photos of the same excellence as the journalistic shots he'd seen in Kitty's portfolio—images of Bedouin family life and historical cityscapes bursting with respect and understated talent.

Amanda huffed at him, but he ignored her. "This is a family wedding, not a circus. I want to see quality photographs that won't be leaked to the media."

He turned to Kitty then wished he hadn't. Luminous brown eyes shone back at him with a lingering hint of amusement that had his breath catching in his throat. She was beautiful.

Make that three female threats to his equilibrium.

No. That was nonsense thinking. He was never attracted to work colleagues. He wasn't in the business of creating his own mayhem.

"I have a contract with Kitty. It includes my supervision." He nodded at Kitty, keeping his gaze carefully on her chin—he'd look at nothing above or below it to distract him.

"Please complete a series of portraits now. They will be our baseline for the full wedding album."

Kitty barely nodded as her demeanor sobered.

He moved to the doorway and watched as she swiveled in a slow circle, surveying the room.

Her lively face, when she turned his way, was subdued in thought. No longer animated by humor or the anger she had used to counter-attack him when they hammered out their contract.

Her mouth formed a soft pout of concentration. Beautiful without the artifice of makeup. Too late, he forgot he was only there to watch her work.

She had already removed her beret but now started to undress as she moved, apparently oblivious of him.

She slowly unwrapped her woolens in obvious response to the heat of the room. The belt at her slender waist, a wide green textured-leather affair with an oversized silver buckle, was cinched tighter as the buckle was eased and then released.

He swallowed, suddenly thirsty as his body responded with an unwelcome increase of tension.

Next, she dropped the belt gently onto the floor beside her camera bag, with barely a glance.

The woolen wrap-coat flapped open, and she pushed it aside, her hands spanning her waist as she looked critically at the furniture in the room.

She drew a curtain and moved a chair. Unhurried. Proficient.

Standing back, still lost in her set-up plans, she shed the coat completely and let it fall in a raspberry red pool beside the belt.

She reminded him of a Christmas present, red and green, multi-wrapped to frustrate and excite the lucky recipient.

He groaned. That was the sort of Redmond thinking he never indulged in. The sort of thinking his father would have said aloud and laughed, the center of attention. Drinks all around, live-for-the-moment sort of thinking.

Risk-everything-you-worked-for thinking.

Rosco frowned.

Kitty's next layer of clothing was some sort of see-through, loose-weave top, falling off one shoulder and doing nothing to hide the skintight black leggings and tank top beneath it.

He couldn't take his eyes off that smooth, slender shoulder. A sudden desire to know what that creamy skin felt like wound his tension up another notch.

The camera came off next—a heavy professional model and perfect for the job, Rosco was forced to admit. Kitty looped it carefully over her head and checked it thoroughly.

Suddenly, that quiet sense of concentration was replaced by one of frenetic energy as Kitty set up the equipment she needed. She motioned for Amanda to stay in the chair where she was, then she stood back to assess her composition and nodded briskly.

She looked excited and totally immersed in her work. The muscles in his right leg started to cramp, but he resisted massaging the familiar, old-injury ache, a sure sign of tension he refused to acknowledge. He couldn't take his eyes off the action.

Kitty stalked backward on those impossibly high heels toward the coffee table, her eyes never leaving Amanda. With quick, fluid movements, she peeled off her last layer of decent clothing, then scooped up her long dark hair and twisted it into a haphazard knot. It settled low on the creamy skin of her neck, above the skintight black-clad length of her.

There was nothing between her body and Rosco's imagination. He ran a quick finger around the suddenly constricting neckline of his own shirt collar. He was hot. The fire, he decided, had been an unnecessary autumn indulgence.

Kitty crouched low with her camera to match the lens to Amanda's eye level.

She clicked repeatedly, murmuring directions to Amanda, moving forward and back to get the portrait compositions she wanted.

Rosco admired her natural balance, perfectly in control of those high heels. Her long legs lithe and supple. Her breasts a palm-sized swell beneath her cotton top.

His jaw locked tight on another annoying wave of desire—he usually appreciated far more subtle female attractions. Women who knew how to cover up, their clothes expensive, tasteful, and rarely leaving their bodies in public. Nothing like Kitty's take-me-or-leave-me skintight black. Her unselfconsciously sexy black.

And he only ever dated women as focused on their careers as he was on his own, women who weren't looking for commitment and children. No one who sparked his emotions. His sisters, niece, and the late mother he owed everything to, were all the women he needed in his life. All he had time to care for.

"Relax, Rosco." Fiona sighed, interrupting his thoughts as she came up behind him. "Everything is going to be fine. Mom would have loved Amanda's wedding plans. She always said her own wedding was a big extravagant party. She'd want you to enjoy it all."

Rosco threw her a quick smile in response. He wouldn't dream of hurting his mother's memory, but look where infatuation with their party-loving father had left her. Left them all.

Widowed and debt-laden. A single mother with three young children and little experience of the ailing publishing business she had inherited.

No. He wouldn't trust anyone else with the rebuilt welfare of this family. *His* family.

Risk management was his plan for this wedding. The photographs would be perfect and totally private. This event was not going to degenerate into a public spectacle.

"That will do," he said to Kitty, moving from the doorway. "Show me the screen."

Kitty rose slowly, flicking through the shots, obviously looking for a superior one to show him first.

She held the camera out for him to view the screen, and he felt the blood-pumping pull of her. The temptation of spontaneity, of bare, willowy arms and softly swelling breasts, of her own particular brand of determined confidence.

He leaned in, aware of her soft, flowery perfume, and found excellent headshots of his sister.

He flicked through the shots slowly as Amanda looked over his shoulder.

"I love them," said Amanda. "I told you they'd be wonderful, Rosco." She punched his arm, laughing.

He nodded briefly at Kitty. "Good." He wasn't losing control with too much praise. "I'll expect the same standard for the entire wedding. Full-length portraits and group compositions."

He handed back her camera, careful not to touch her as she stood beside him in what he considered a state of undress. "I'll still be personally supervising all photography. We'll need to discuss the composition requirements of the best man, who uses a wheelchair— "

Amanda silenced him with a wave of her hand as her cell phone signaled a new message. "It's Titania. She's through customs and in her limo. She'll be here in an hour."

Rosco's irritation level soared. Even her name got under his skin. It wasn't the woman herself; he didn't know her. It was all the nonsense around her.

"I don't want her here."

Amanda's face fell before she rounded on him, as he knew she would. What was wrong with him today? He usually managed his sister more strategically.

"You're not my father."

Heaven forbid. "No, but I am custodian of Mother's business. You know I can't afford sensational publicity ruining the Sandford Palace contract."

He didn't bother to hide his groan of annoyance. He wanted Amanda to enjoy her wedding, but this meeting with Titania at his home wasn't going to include him. The paparazzi were not going to have any reason to insinuate a pop star into his private life.

He wasn't going to allow himself to be paraded in the press like the string of Titania's past conquests. His businesses relied on investment integrity, not meaningless media notoriety.

He absorbed another glare from his sister and flicked off his anger, replacing it with the familiar power of action. "Amanda, of course you must enjoy your visit with Titania."

He meant it, but he wasn't going to be trapped by circumstances. "I'll leave you to your wedding tea party. I won't be here. I'll ask Frank to bring the car around."

"Kitty," he said, choosing not to look at her barely-dressed curves as he punched his driver's number into his cell. "Get dressed. We're leaving together."

He'd get her out and then get her some suitable clothes. It was time to cover her up.

"Your confidentiality and anonymity continue to have my guarantee as long as you follow my instructions when we get outside."

He'd have to trust her to face the cameras again as his decoy. And this time—no touching.

Chapter Three

Kitty had no time to process Rosco's demand before he snatched up their contract from the chair where she'd left it. "I'll copy this for you. Keep us both aware of our expectations."

She bristled as he turned on his heel and left them, allowing no opportunity for discussion.

But Amanda just grinned at her brother's retreating back. "He always has to have the last word," she whispered with an affectionate blend of irritation and respect.

Kitty watched him stride from the room, his infuriating confidence detracting nothing at all from the walk-away view. His perfect tailoring precisely outlining his masculine… attributes. *Perfect butt* were words she shouldn't think.

Rosco was her employer. Full stop. And an alarming one, now that he required her to face the media scrum again. The thought of walking through a gaggle of photographers was already crowding out her professional pleasure in landing this contract.

There was no way he could guarantee anything.

She stifled a sigh, returning her attention to the bride-to-be, and passed over her camera. "Click through all the shots," she said to both Amanda and Fiona, who had joined her sister standing by the fire. "Select any you want me to print for you."

The two sisters, so alike with their long blond hair and friendly confidence, became happily absorbed in the gallery. "Mom would have loved these," Kitty heard Fiona say with a fond smile in her voice.

Kitty turned away from their fond memories to slowly collect her equipment and repack her bag.

She needed to think.

This house, so like her mother's, kept flicking up memories she didn't want.

And Rosco, so appealing in his sharp suit. She needed to remind herself how *unappealing* men in suits could be when you got to know them. Her mother's party friends had taught her that.

Her childhood held little of the care and respect she heard in the Redmond family. The image of Cara, her blond curls soft against Rosco's dark jacket, lingered in her thoughts. And envy stabbed her. Envy of a little girl who was loved by a man behind a safe family door.

Then the moment passed as she felt Rosco return, stirring the female vibe with his faintly disapproving masculinity. He didn't even enter the room, just propped himself, long and lean, against the door frame.

He ignored Kitty and commanded Amanda's attention. "Update me on Titania's security arrangements. You know the media will be following everything about this wedding with her in the picture."

"Don't start lecturing me about that again."

"It's important, Amanda. You need to consider the wider implications for our family and business."

"Titania has it all covered. She isn't attending the rehearsal in Wheatbridge Village. She's laying a false trail suggesting the wedding is here in London, and on the actual day she will have her own security to ensure the paps can't get near the venues."

Rosco moved closer to her, his voice a low burr of frustration. "Too late. The paps, as you so chummily call them, are already at our front door."

Amanda clapped her hands. "It just makes everything more exciting." She grinned up at her brother. "It's all under control. Titania's people are experts in handling these situations. You worry too much."

Kitty watched Rosco's cheeks flush a very irritated shade of crimson and felt a twinge of sympathy for him as she tried to hide her own concerns about the personal exposure.

"Kitty has no experience with this level of media attention your wedding is generating." He dragged his hand through his hair and turned the full force of his authority onto Kitty.

"You will have to consider your every move over the next two days. If you have any doubts at all about your ability to handle that, you can leave right now, and I'll find someone else." Maybe she wasn't hiding her own uneasiness as well as she hoped.

"I have international, award-winning photography experience and a signed contract with you." She'd hold on to that contract like a life raft to ensure she stayed in this job long enough to prove her worth.

He faced her, combative with his feet apart.

"I've already told you," Kitty emphasized, anticipating another strike against her trustworthiness. "I did not bring the paparazzi to your door. I do not live in the media world. They don't know me."

Heaven forbid Trinity St. George should ever disprove that. But he had assured her the wretched woman who knew her childhood secrets had nothing to do with this wedding.

"Furthermore" —she snapped her small light reflector

closed and pointed it at him as he opened his mouth to continue what felt like a threatening assault on her contract—"I have worked in many politically unstable areas of the world and fully understand the politics of media attention and diplomacy."

"I doubt your experience has prepared you for the duplicity of the paparazzi." He undid his jacket and thrust his hands on his hips, leaning toward her.

"You're quite wrong." Phew. The impact of his arrogance and the sudden view of his taut, crisp-shirted body, threatened to sabotage her. "My extensive experience has honed my skills—forward planning, security, and strict "no comment" policies apply to all high-risk situations."

She sounded like an over-hyped, best-deal-ever commercial, but when cornered, she talked. It had worked for her in the past, and right now words crowded her senses. The contract was secure, but her employer's respect still seemed elusive.

He barely nodded, eyes cool, as his glare swept over her and stopped at the pile of clothes at her feet. "Get dressed. Frank is ten minutes away."

No comment in high-risk situations played across her mind like a blinking neon sign as she turned away. Time to be quiet. And to once again shake off the way his cool glare churned up her childhood shame, especially in this house.

She completed packing her bag, threw on her clothes, and jammed her beret onto her head, all without another word passing between them.

Amanda broke the silence by handing back the camera along with a request for all the photos to be emailed so she could look at them with Andrew, her fiancé.

Kitty nodded, capped the camera, and looped it over her head, drawing on the familiar feel of it around her neck to bolster her courage.

"Hide that camera in your bag." Rosco frowned at her.

That made sense—it did advertise her role here—so she complied without comment, and then Rosco moved forward to take the bag from her.

"My plan is to get us both out of here and away from the Titania visit."

"So you leave with another woman. Me." She glared at him, ignoring Amanda's amused glances between them. "How does that protect my anonymity?"

"Keep your head down and say nothing."

The contract flashed before her eyes again. She needed to hold on to it. Even if he was using her as an anti-Titania decoy, he obviously wasn't going to admit it.

"Amanda, get Kitty some large sunglasses to wear. That will have to do until we can get her some suitable clothing."

There it was again, judgment of her appearance. Her skin prickled with annoyance. What was he thinking, dictating her appearance? Surely way beyond employer rights. Was the man actually ashamed to be seen with her?

"What do you mean by 'suitable'?"

"Professional. Covered up."

She wasn't conceding that, even if it did echo her own regret about wardrobe choices. "My clothes don't affect the quality of my work."

"They do affect your anonymity. Your clothes draw attention to you." He racked a another quick glance at her body. "Follow me." He turned on his heel.

But he didn't get out of the room before the front doorbell rang—long, loud, and strident.

"Ah," said Amanda as she rummaged in her handbag and produced very celebrity-looking shades for Kitty. "That will be Aunt Ethel. You can practice a few of the group shots Rosco mentioned earlier." She winked wickedly. "I'll get him to join us for them." She paused a beat. "He'll be thrilled."

"There's no time for that," Rosco barked as the doorbell shrilled again.

Kitty stilled at the urgency in its tone and watched it have exactly the opposite effect on Rosco.

He strode out to the foyer and wrenched opened the door. An older woman almost fell into the house as Rosco once more slammed the door on paparazzi cameras.

"Good to see you, lad," said the woman with a no-nonsense look about her stout boots and tweed coat.

"Aunt Ethel," Rosco said, kissing her cheek with scrupulous politeness. "What news do you bring from the circus out there?"

"You and Titania." His aunt slapped his shoulder in satisfaction. "About time, lad. I'll just pop back out and confirm you're a couple. Give the business a boost in the press, too."

Rosco groaned and placed his body in front of the door. "Complete nonsense," he told his aunt.

"That's a shame. She's a lovely gal. Never fear, I'll match you up with one of the other bridesmaids at the wedding."

Kitty watched as Rosco stood ramrod straight, every muscle on guard.

"That won't be possible," he said as Kitty noticed Amanda and Fiona, who had joined them, catch each other's eye.

Fiona appeared quietly amused by the battle in front of them. But Amanda was struggling to contain her laughter. She doubled over, pretending to inspect the heel of her shoe, and shook with silent mirth.

Ethel, oblivious to their presence behind her, continued a tirade of romantic advice as she faced her nephew squarely, her handbag over her arm. Rosco took it all without comment, but a slow flush crept up his neck as his good manners obviously struggled against his exasperation.

"I'm sorry, Aunt. But I really won't be free at the wedding," he repeated. "I'll be supervising the photographer."

"That's typical of you, Rosco," she said. "All work and no play. Been that way ever since you were a boy."

A flash of pity warmed Kitty's lingering annonyance. How awful to have family meddling in his personal life and undervaluing his work ethic.

Rosco didn't comment further, but he didn't deny it, either, as he turned to Kitty.

"Aunt, this is Kitty Mayfair. She's inexperienced but basically technically proficient. We're leaving now to prepare for tomorrow's rehearsal photography at the Village."

Basically technically proficient. His description triggered rebellion in Kitty's heart. Her professional proficiency was her identity.

She shook Ethel's hand as resentment curdled her blood, and she couldn't help throwing a furious glance at Rosco. "Yes, I've a lot of supervised preparation work to do."

Ethel eyed her suspiciously, her gaze flicking between them. "I'm beginning to get the picture here," she said, with obvious amusement at her own photography joke. "It's about time, Rosco. How long have you been working with this lovely young thing?"

Kitty recognized an opportunity to get some control back when she saw one. He needed to be taught a lesson.

And she decided, then, he needed saving from the sort of family interference she would loathe for herself, and found she inexplicably couldn't bear for him.

So before Rosco could reply she linked a possessive arm with his and worked hard to relax her face into a contented smile. "Our collaboration is very recent. I'm very grateful for Rosco's guidance."

She ignored his rigid resistance to her touch and risked a small coquettish smile up into his ice-blue eyes.

"Why, that's wonderful news," cried Ethel, spreading her

arms wide to embrace them both.

Rosco swallowed, painfully it seemed, and Kitty had to work hard to contain her amusement. Something Amanda was failing at miserably. She clapped her hand over her mouth and fled back into the living room.

At last Rosco found his voice. It was a little ragged to Kitty's ears, but that gruff Irish burr could possibly be confused with passion if you were a smitten elderly aunt who didn't know the truth.

"It's a purely professional relationship, Aunt," he said, withdrawing his arm from Kitty's. "And I'd appreciate it if you kept that inappropriate gleam in your eye to yourself. It's wedding business."

"Of course, my dear." She winked at her nephew and adjusted her handbag purposefully in the crook of her arm. "Your secret is safe with me. I'll go join the girls for tea."

"Women," Rosco grunted, giving Kitty the full frosty chill of his CEO power as they watched Ethel follow Amanda and Fiona into the living room.

Alone in the foyer, he turned to Kitty. "This ridiculous innuendo ends immediately after the wedding." He pointed an emphatic index finger at her. "Do you understand?"

"Absolutely." She curbed the impulse to salute. Relationships, loving mothers, and interfering aunts weren't for her. Not for real. They were all totally outside her experience.

"So what's in this farce for you?" The suspicion in his tone, unpleasantly close to a sneer, challenged her integrity. It snaked under her skin, like the sleazy threat of the paparazzi, and pushed her to remember all the childhood scandal she'd risen above. Scandal that Rosco Redmond's strict moral code would find shameful.

"I'm impulsive. And a born rescuer," she whispered, voicing the truth of a child who'd shouldered too many adult worries in a house so uncomfortably similar to his. "All I want for the next two days is an atmosphere without arguments so I can produce perfect photos."

She held his gaze, watched cynicism linger in the dark navy depths of his eyes, and wished again she *was* wearing corporate clothes to match his tailored authority. "Plus, you deserved to know how it felt to be dragged into innuendo. We still have the paparazzi to face."

"We do." He sighed, and his face softened a little, the cynicism lightening into what she hoped was respect. "I think you have enough sense to handle them, Kitty Mayfair. They can't be more difficult than Aunt Ethel."

She thought there was a small smile in his tone as he picked up her camera bag and gave the street outside one last check through the security glass. "Take care of yourself out there. Walk beside me, keep your head down, and walk straight to the car. No talking."

She nodded and put on the glamorous sunglasses Amanda had given her, fluffed her hair around her face, and stood facing the front door. Once again she resolutely ignored the familiar grandeur around her and the memories it stirred, willing herself not to look up the stairs, not to acknowledge the dull ache developing in her heart.

She couldn't wait to get away from here, away from the soft Irish accent with the suggestion of a warm smile she was tempted to pretend was just for her. The last couple of hours suddenly felt like a week.

Rosco opened the door and her heart plummeted to her boots. Paparazzi swarmed over the steps between them and their ride, a black limousine with darkened windows.

Rosco shouldered his way down the steps, saying nothing to the calls for information about Titania.

Kitty placed her feet just behind his, watching the smart black leather of his shoes clip their way toward the sanctuary of the car.

They almost made it.

The paps crowded arounded them, and Kitty could see Rosco's hand reach for the rear door handle. Two of the guys with cameras snatched the opportunity to separate them and Kitty found herself cornered between the cameras and Rosco's broad shoulders.

"Hello, love," called one of the men, his raised visor revealing a puffy, lined face squashed into his black cycle helmet. She recognized him from earlier. He was persistent. "You going to the wedding, then?"

"What's your connection then, love?" asked the other, lifting his camera to her face.

She ducked her head farther toward her chest, trusting her anonymity to her hair and sunglasses, and thinking fast. If they wanted a story she'd give them one, and hopefully make her own photography assignment easier as well.

"I'm just a lucky wedding guest. London is so romantic."

"Lucky you," agreed the helmeted pap in an oily voice. "So you'll be partying with the famous pop star. You look very pretty, love. A bit like Titania herself, from a distance, anyway."

"Goodness, thanks. She's gorgeous isn't she?" Just one last false clue. "She'll be here on Saturday. The wedding's in the evening. You should see the house. They've started decorating already. Gold and purple everywhere."

Kitty tapped her fingers to her lips and shrugged with a little giggle. "Oops. Too much information."

"That's enough," Rosco rumbled in her ear. Just loud enough for the paps to hear, she realized.

Kitty felt his body move to shield hers as he reached the car door to wrench it open at last, and then she tumbled into a luxurious expanse of black leather.

Rosco joined her, closing the door on the noisy street

scene and cocooning her in blessed silence. She slid along the seat opposite him so there was no chance of their legs touching, and pressed her hands together to stop the shaky feelings starting in her stomach.

She'd spoken when she shouldn't have, but time would tell if her plan worked.

"That was quite a performance," Rosco said as his driver steered skillfully through the paparazzi still clicking at the darkened windows of the car.

He was back in CEO mode, and Kitty couldn't tell what he really thought. She'd have to pretend she didn't care.

"One last task and then I'll leave you to prepare for your journey to Wheatbridge Village tomorrow. The rehearsal is at midday. I'll email all instructions."

He selected a business card from his wallet and passed it to Kitty. "I've made an appointment for you at Cynthia's Boutique, one of my mother's favorite stores."

His gaze flicked over her, judging again, as it had when she'd first rang his doorbell. Was that really only a couple of hours ago?

"I have requested a small range of suitable outfits be available to you for the wedding. Please choose one you like. All chargeable to your contract expenses. Frank will then drive you home."

"No thank you. I'll take the tube." There would be no anonymity in a flashy limousine, and she craved a bit of normality to prepare for her days ahead as a supervised photographer.

"As you wish. Choose your outfit wisely."

"Wisely." She huffed at him, cross, and too hyped to hide it. "I can dress myself."

"Not for this assignment. I require a totally professional image now that you've drawn additional attention to us by speaking to the media."

"That's rich." She enjoyed the pun, throwing her hands up to encompass the plush interior of the limo, his crisp tailoring, and the very fact that they were being chauffeured through the busy London traffic. "I'm not responsible for being *dragged* into this situation."

"I'm not revisiting that discussion. We have a contract. We have been photographed together. We will see those images published."

"Not my fault." She felt hot now, claustrophobic, in the plush leather car, the tautly muscled length of him, tensed for combat, filling her senses.

"Fault isn't the issue." He squared his shoulders and pinned her with a cold, impersonal glance. "Your arrival at my house may be a timely decoy, but it needs to be managed. I had no intention of being seen in public with Titania, but I wasn't seeking to replace her, either. To control any future images of us together, I want you dressed discreetly."

"Yes, sir." She looked down at the business card he'd given her and couldn't wait for the car to get her there. To escape him and the feeling of being judged and found lacking.

She bit her lip as resentment seethed through her. All she'd wanted at the beginning of the day was a photography contract. She hadn't asked for these complications, and she wasn't handing over control of her wardrobe to anyone.

Chapter Four

The next day Rosco watched Kitty drive under the stone archway of the Wheatbridge Inn and bump to a gentle stop on the cobbles. She was thirty minutes late for their appointment prior to the wedding rehearsal.

Not a good start, as it was only a two-hour drive from London.

Her car was a fanciful little vintage Citroën Dolly, oddly fitting in this picture-perfect Cotswolds country village with its gently undulating hills and dry-stone walls.

Rosco shoved his smart phone into his shirt pocket and marched toward her.

Kitty stepped out of the car as he approached, and he almost broke his stride, his chest constricted at the sight of her, his reprimand dying on his lips.

She dazzled in hot pink. A tight long-sleeved T-shirt just skimming the top of her skinny jeans.

And printed across her chest was a large juicy slice of lime. He tried not to look. But he was a citrus man from way back.

She looked as fresh and enticing as her T-shirt.

"Cute fruit," he said.

"Thanks." She smiled and pulled the fabric away from her body to look down at the design.

The movement accentuated her curves, and the lime seemed to suck all moisture from his mouth.

"It's for my sister's restaurant, Fuchsia and Lime." She gave a happy little bounce. "They're new. We're thrilled with them."

"Ah ha," he managed, with an encouraging nod.

"It's selling well, even with the advertising slogan on the back." She turned, twisting her hips so he could read the words while she watched him over her shoulder.

He licked his lips. "Fuschia & Lime," he obediently recited the first line snuggled into the curve of her waist. "Dawn 'til dark for fine food and wine," he croaked, his throat parched beyond speech.

"Too cheesy for you?" She chewed the corner of her bottom lip.

"No. No. It all looks grand to me." That was the trouble; it did look grand. She looked grand. "But we had agreed you'd be wearing something from the store I sent you to." He stepped back and away from her.

"Sorry, early morning duties at my sister's restaurant and no time to change. But I've got my wedding outfit." She grinned at him and stretched into the car for a distinctive silver garment bag. At full stretch, her T-shirt once again parted company with her jeans.

Damn. He needed to get a grip and concentrate on wedding business and security priorities. He didn't trust the way his focus could waver when Kitty appeared.

She unzipped the bag to reveal a long skirt and short jacket. They were black and perfectly tailored—and nothing like Kitty herself.

That was good because this lively, hot-pink Kitty seemed to threaten the tight rein he had on what he thought of as *Redmond thinking*. He wasn't about to be swayed by her obvious enjoyment of life. He could never allow himself to be tempted, especially by an employee, and find he was in any way like his father.

"Appropriate choice."

"I thought you'd approve. Cynthia was very helpful."

He looked at her sharply, as a slight teasing tone in her voice activated his female manipulation alarm.

Kitty turned away to remove more of her gear from the car, and he allowed his annoyance to build. The woman should dress with more caution. She knew they were under possible media threat. Hadn't she learned anything from yesterday?

He bent down to pick up her small collection of bags. It was all the impractical little trunk of her dinky little car could hold. Who drove a car with no storage? "Do you have everything you need for the job?"

"Of course." She wrapped the garment bag over one arm and shouldered a folding tripod as he led her into the inn.

"You travel light."

"Years of experience."

Her tone again snipped at his control. He was in charge. "That's worthless if you're late." He wasn't listening to her or to the temptation to keep looking at that damn slice of lime on her chest. "Today and tomorrow are under my direction."

He placed her luggage in the empty reception area and rang the bell. "I'll leave you to check in. Join me in the small conference room in ten minutes. I've ordered refreshments."

And cover up, he wanted to say again. But that would tell her it continued to bother him, and he wasn't going to make that tactical error.

He left her without a backward glance, walked to the conference room, and unlocked the door, returning to his papers strewn across the table.

The time waiting for Kitty hadn't been wasted. He'd liaised with his driver, Frank, who was driving incognito in a rental car and ensured Rosco that his sisters and niece had safely, and privately, arrived at their late mother's country house.

It had been only two years since leukemia claimed her life, and the house was just as she had left it. His sisters used it as a country retreat, and they had no plans to sell it.

Their privacy would be well supported by the local villagers, but it was the big city media that continued to worry him.

He clicked through a variety of online social news sites, as he had a dozen times since the ambush on him and Kitty the day before.

There had been nothing earlier, but now he discovered grainy images of his city house behind an enormous headline: "It's a Gold and Purple Bridesmaid Dress for Titania."

His jaw tightened as a close-up photo of him and Kitty in a tight embrace was circled beside the headline.

Titania was the main subject of the article—not that a few scraps of misinformation deserved to be called an article. But the byline under the small photograph posed the gallingly inane question, "Who's Romancing Rosco?"

Kitty looked cornered, and it caught at his heart. Spinning him back to his anger at the paparazzi's intrusion.

He'd been so fixated on not being linked to Titania, he'd allowed himself to use an employee.

However, she had still accepted the job and signed their contract. She'd also voluntarily misled his aunt and had appeared to enjoy that almost as much as his sister.

And as he read farther down the text, the success of Kitty's false trail impressed him, with the words "the lucky guest's insider details of the London wedding." forcing him into a reluctant grin

A heavily embroidered version of Kitty's brief comments filled the screen. Some "journalist" obviously interviewed their own keyboard long into the night. Any problem he might have with the ethics of that evaporated as the gushing words made the London location of Amanda's wedding sound cloyingly authentic.

Titania's arrival at the house just minutes after his departure with Kitty was heavily photographed in associated articles and further corroborated the fiction.

This whole fiasco was working as well as he could have hoped.

Kitty had showed some gumption, and he allowed the beginnings of a grudging respect. He enjoyed a fight. A fair one. And Kitty may just be an asset in this guerrilla war designed to deprive him of the prize he wanted for his mother's company.

It was worth fighting for. Worth winning.

Kitty bounced into the room, looking at her cell phone and commanding his attention, her wardrobe as unbusinesslike as ever. "We've made the gossip sites. I told you we'd be freeze-framed into a hug. But you can't tell who I am."

"I've seen. You're as anonymous as you were before we met." He wasn't getting into the hug debate again, but her smile was infectious, and her elation lifted his spirits even further. "Great work. You thought on your feet."

"Anytime, boss." Again that feminine, flirty flick-off as she took the seat opposite him. "What's next? I thought you promised food."

"It's ordered." He watched her thumbing her way around the internet with a youthful dexterity that made him feel ancient, even though there must be only five years between them. He hated the whole "live online" thing of social media, the trigger-happy way people revealed their personal lives.

There was no permanent erase button.

His earlier concerns about the media splash she'd made came rushing back. His actions had been uncharacteristically lacking in caution when he'd pulled her into his house. And later, when he'd pushed her into his limo.

His motives had been almost entirely selfish. To preserve his business integrity. To avoid any association with Titania ruining his chance of winning the Sandford Palace contract.

And that was what niggled at him now as he watched Kitty intensely scanning her screen. However upbeat she was, he'd seen vulnerability and a lick of fear in her face as they'd escaped into the limo.

Her posture hunched, her face pinched… He hadn't questioned it at the time. It was understandable. He'd felt hounded himself.

But what was she afraid of? What was she hiding?

There was that odd comment about growing up in a house like his. What childhood situation had provided her with a privileged home?

And her website and social media pages showed no personal information. He approved the restraint, but it made her an unknown entity.

She had proved excellent for foiling the Titania connection and for lightly managing his aunt's matchmaking. But what about the Sandford Palace contract? The wedding would be over tomorrow, and with his supervision he knew the photos would be excellent. But the Titania-generated media intrusion had created a chink in his usually intact social armor.

He would still be reliant on Kitty's discretion. It would be prudent to know more about her.

"How did you manage last night after our confrontation?"

"No problems." She stopped scanning her cell screen with obvious reluctance. "Why do you ask?"

"Employer concern."

"I said no problems, boss."

He gritted his teeth against her continued use of the word "boss." The flippant dismissal ceased to be charming.

"Have you been ambushed by paparazzi before?"

"No." She speared him with a suspicious look, and he carefully blanked his face. She'd stopped the flirting and was giving him her full attention. "Were they still there when you arrived home?"

"I spent the night in the on-site flat at work after an hour at the gym." His personal trainer had worked late, and the intense workout had burned off much of his surplus adrenaline from the day. Otherwise sleep would have been impossible. The gym was also an excellent alibi. If he was there, he wasn't with Titania.

"I had chocolate and red wine with my sister," Kitty said.

"The media drove you to drink?"

"Yep."

He must have looked shocked, because she frowned and then softened it with a small twinkly smile. "It's okay, boss. I didn't get drunk. No issues with my work skills today." She held her hands out in front of her. "See, no shaking."

She was back to teasing him. Managing him. The flippancy didn't gel with the focus he'd seen in her work yesterday. Suspicion made him hyper-vigilant. He had a lot at stake here.

"What about this morning, Kitty? You were late. Were you followed?"

Chapter Five

Kitty's skin goosed up as Rosco's gaze concentrated on her. Was the man a mind reader?

Fortunately, the arrival of their lunch allowed her to stall for time. Sandwiches and tea were beautifully presented on wooden platters, with a sharply modern teapot to match the stylish chrome-and-glass furnished meeting room.

She faced him across the table and felt twelve years old again and in trouble at school. Back then she'd talked too much. Now, she wasn't going to repeat that mistake.

"No." It was the truth. She had no proof she had been followed.

"You're sure?"

"Yes." She ramped up the confidence in her tone and crossed her fingers under the table, hoping he couldn't actually read her mind.

She'd keep her disquiet to herself. It hadn't occurred to her to suspect she would be followed until she'd noticed a green car once too often. It had stopped with her at a breakfast café and seemed to keep just behind her on the motorway.

But when she turned off toward the village she hadn't seen it again.

"Why would I be followed? I'm not important and no one knows who I am." She was probably imagining it, anyway. Yesterday had stirred up more childhood memories than she was prepared to admit, even to herself.

"That's grand. I was worried for you."

"Grand," said Kitty, rolling the word on her tongue. She wasn't convinced his concern was for her. More likely for his precious business. But the softness of his Irish "grand" curled around her heart somehow. Foolish, but she suddenly wanted to know about it. "There you go being Irish again. Your sisters don't sound like you."

He pursed his lips, and an awkward silence lengthened between them as she reached for a sandwich and nibbled at a frill of lettuce overflowing from the creamy filling.

"I'm sorry, that was inappropriately personal. I guess we're on paid-contract time now. Although you did comment on my T-shirt."

He began to pour two cups of tea. "My father was Irish," he said quietly, and with unmistakeable reluctance. "We all moved to England before the girls were old enough to acquire an accent. I haven't quite lost mine, I'm told."

His father. Of course. Clear to anyone who'd grown up with a family. Obviously not her. She'd touched a nerve when she hadn't meant to. "I'm sorry I asked. Of course, you will all be thinking of your father at this time."

"Aye. A daughter should be able to rely on her father to look after her at her wedding," he said, with a touch of the brogue roughening his words.

"In an ideal world." She nodded as diplomatically as possible, but personally she couldn't see the need for either the wedding or the father.

It was just like her to blunder into taboo subjects.

Rosco handed her a cup of tea, and their fingers brushed with a fizz of heat she couldn't control. A reaction to the arresting combination of his charming accent and smile that had no place in their working relationship.

Kitty looked away, biting into her sandwich and dousing the heat with the cold reality of their situation. She needed this job for her financial future. Rosco needed a professional wedding album and her discretion as his decoy love interest to protect him from the paps. That was more than enough to concentrate on.

"It's a complicated time. Nothing ideal about it. Your support with the media was appreciated." He was back to business, too.

"Glad to help." Her remembered anger at the paps scooted along her veins. "They were vile. It's totally unjust to hound people the way they do." She took a breath, watched him watching her, and pulled back on her passion. "It's an unethical misuse of photography," she said, hoping he didn't ask for any more personal reasons for her distaste. Just because he was her employer and she was supporting his privacy didn't mean he had to know *her* life story.

"Unprofessional. Yes." He took a sip of tea. "Persistent? Unfortunately, also a yes," he continued, and then bit down on a man-sized beef sandwich.

Kitty looked away, diverted from their shared cause by the closeness of Rosco in his smart navy suit and crisp blue shirt. Perfect with those matching blue eyes.

It was a fine autumn day, with the trees outside just turning to russet and gold. A ray of pale sunshine shone through the window beside them and glinted the same tones in Rosco's warm brown hair.

"You're worried they'll crash the wedding, aren't you?" she said, dragging her thoughts back to the task at hand and away from fanciful ideas of sunshine and a handsome man.

"I don't worry. I prepare. I'm vigilant." He speared her with a hard glance and took another bite of food.

Kitty waited while he ate, fueling his resolve, and her throat constricted as he swallowed. She'd felt an exciting rush of adventure when she successfully duped the press. But she didn't fancy having to do it again. Risking her privacy.

"We're safe today. Your performance seems to have concentrated attention back in London. But Titania is a risk we can't calculate."

"I'm sure you have a contingency plan for tomorrow, Rosco."

"Of course I do," he said, a determined glint in his eye revealing a hint of something like her secret excitement. Interesting.

"Good. We can concentrate on the wedding prep now." She wanted to keep her professionalism front and center to ensure he would agree to view her future project submissions.

"Very good," he said. "Back to business. Your expertise and my supervision."

She worked hard not to groan and took a gulp of tea. She'd swallow the supervision jibe to keep the peace.

"To a matchmaking-free partnership," she said, unable to resist annoying him back. "Ethel thinks I need you for photography supervision, and I promise to keep you busy whenever confetti looks like it's being tossed your way." She grinned at him. "Can't think of anything worse than being married off myself."

"Me, either. Not to any woman," he said with exaggerated horror. He emphasized the "any" in a way she read was to ensure she knew he was including her.

She smothered a smile at this uncharacteristic glimpse into his private life, and resolutely ignored a ridiculous stab of hurt in her heart at his implied rejection of her.

"No one," he continued. "Not the aunts' idea of a domestic

goddess, however well intentioned. And especially not with Titania. Publicity hell, that one."

"Quite an issue for you," she said, considering him over her tea cup. "You haven't strung that many words together since we met."

"All part of this wedding madness," he said, avoiding her gaze. "There's more to it than you need to know." He ended the topic and was back to his bossy business best. "I'm still concerned about the group work at the wedding. The best man uses a wheelchair. You'll need to accommodate that height differential in your work."

"I was an official photographer for the last Para-Olympics." She could do business-speak Rosco-style anytime he wanted. "It's a composition challenge but not a problem. You can see some of my athletes' group shots on my website."

He merely nodded curtly as he tidied the paperwork spread out on the table into his briefcase. Another test passed.

"But I'm keen to hear your ideas," she said, surprised how much she meant it. Not that ideas meant advice. But this was a very personal event for his family, and getting it right meant keeping her ego and prejudices out of the picture. "What is your itinerary for this afternoon?"

"I want to start here at the inn. The reception will be in their main event area, which includes outside seating leading down to the river."

He led Kitty out of the room and walked purposefully through the complex with that masculine stride of his.

The inn and its event facilities looked stunning. And expensive. They had the charm and character of bygone years combined with all the modern conveniences any wedding event would need. Photographically, it posed no challenges for Kitty.

"Just speeches and cake cutting here, Rosco?"

"Yes. And more table shots than usual would be good,

too. The rest of the chairs will be the same height as Russell's wheelchair. Not that I want to hide the wheelchair. It isn't a problem for me or for Russell. I just want the best photos."

Kitty checked his face to see if he was teasing her about her group work skills, but she saw only concern for equality and quality. His blue eyes were earnest as they met hers, and she had to fight again against that goosefleshing magnetic pull of him.

She rubbed her arms to warm them. "Where to next?" she asked briskly.

He led her back to the carpark to a black SUV. "We're having our rehearsal at the church in thirty minutes. We have just enough time to get there."

He clipped his safety belt and checked hers before driving off smoothly, his hands strong and capable on the steering wheel.

The hum of the tires on the quiet country road filled the silence between them, and Kitty grew acutely aware of him in the confined space of the car. Workplace attractions were on all the no-no lists. And all males had manly hands and drove cars. Whatever was the matter with her? She looked away from his body, so close to hers, and concentrated on the passing scenery.

The green fields and twisting lanes were beautiful, but it was the history in the dry wall fences and ocassional heritage building she loved the most. When the ruin of an ancient church came into view it demanded to be photographed.

"Stop!" she cried, and he screeched to an immediate halt, flinging his left arm out in front of her to cushion the forward thrust of her body.

"Are you hurt?" he asked, turning to her with concern.

"No." She shook her head, pointing back over her shoulder. "The ruin we passed. Go back."

He gave her an annoyed sort of smile. "Don't do that

again," he said irritably. His arm still rested close to hers, almost touching, protective. "I thought you were in trouble."

"Sorry," she said, chastened and confused that she'd worried him somehow. "I tend to fly off like that when I'm in work mode." He pulled away from her and put the car into reverse. "I guess you don't lose control." It was a statement. She already knew the answer.

He shook his head. "I don't like surprises when I'm driving. I'm not a mind reader."

Good. Just as well he couldn't read her unprofessional thoughts about how cute he was when he was cross.

He checked his watch. "We don't have time for this stop. We need to keep to schedule."

"This ruin is perfect for photos. Amanda would love it."

He gave her an exasperated look and backed the car to the field gate opposite the ruin. Kitty turned again to look out the window and hid a smile. He genuinely did want the best for his sister.

"I've driven past this a hundred times but never really looked at it." He grunted as he leaned over her to get a better view of the ruin, and her mind veered off its professional focus again.

"You're right," he conceded, so close she could smell the subtle citrus of aftershave again. "You've got a good eye."

"Let's get a closer look," she said as she started to unbuckle her seat belt. The gate into the field was obviously unused, stuck open in the grass. "The one remaining arch would frame Amanda beautifully."

He checked his watch again. "No. I'll walk it later."

"Right." She sat back again, folding her arms. "Ethel isn't here. We've only agreed to pretend I need your supervision when she is."

"You might have fooled Ethel into some romantic notion. But between us, I'm still your contracting supervisor.

My family. My responsibility." He pulled back onto the road without another glance in her direction. Heavens, he was infuriating in full head-of-the-family mode.

He drove them directly to the gable-arched porch of the stone church and pulled up behind three cars already parked on the gravel driveway.

Immediately, Kitty was welcomed by Amanda, who introduced her to Andrew, her husband-to-be, and then to Russell, their best man.

Two bridesmaids, Amanda's friends from London, minus Titania, were smiling in welcome. Cara hopped excitedly from foot to foot beside her mother. "I'm going to be a flower girl," she said, swinging a practice basket of garden flowers.

She looked adorable, and Kitty exchanged fond smiles with Fiona and Amanda as their brother marched toward them.

"Thank you for working with Rosco," whispered Amanda. "We know you don't need supervision. But protecting Rosco from the aunts will be one less worry for us. He needs looking after in his own grumpy way."

Amanda rolled her eyes as Rosco swept past them, and Kitty's heart thrilled at the conspiracy between them. She liked Amanda and the way she used humor to manage her brother. Without the complications of a contract and a decoy romance, she would be thoroughly enjoying the friendship blossoming between them. Then the moment evaporated as Rosco called them all to greet the vicar, who was entering the church from behind the altar.

An elderly, cheerful man, he led them all through the service rehearsal at an easy, nerve-calming pace. And he allowed plenty of time for Kitty to plan her shots.

Rosco hovered in her peripheral vision, working hard, she suspected, not to interfere and invite a cheeky put-down from his sister. He obviously got on with Russell and Andrew very well. Heaven help Andrew if he didn't.

There must be a story behind Rosco's acceptance of Amanda's choice of husband. A story that might answer some of her questions about what made Rosco Redmond tick. She needed all the info she could get to work out how best to interest him in her other photographic projects. She was also intrigued to know why his aversion to paparazzi and personal publicity was as fierce as her own.

And, if she were honest with herself, she wanted to know if he was a man worthy of all the heat and bother he seemed to cause her. He took charge again, confirming plans for the next day. Kitty would arrive at the family's country house in plenty of time for some pre-wedding photographs.

Then, with addresses checked and phone numbers exchanged for any last-minute discussions, Rosco ended the get-together. He led Kitty quickly to the car and dropped her back at the inn. He said he had hours of work to catch up on and wished her a rapid good night. Kitty waved good-bye to him with some relief.

In just one day she had become entangled in a web of subterfuge, within the sort of family she had no experience with, and with a man who challenged both her independence and her hormone control.

She was obliged by a contract she knew she was lucky to have, her professional desire to give Amanda the very best wedding album, and her outrage at the paparazzi intrusion.

Add in her fears for her privacy, and the way flashes of humor from bossy-boots Rosco warmed her blood, and she was in way over her head. It was dizzying.

She needed some private time to escape the Redmond family wedding plans. It was just a job, after all.

Chapter Six

The next morning Rosco knocked loudly on Kitty's hotel door and wished he could relax a little. He wanted to talk through any last-minute preparations and to escape the wedding mayhem, in equal measure. Ethel was still harping him about his bachelor status. He'd told her he was leaving to finalize the photography arrangements, then sped away.

Kitty opened the door with one boot on her leg, one boot in her hand. Rosco didn't know where to look.

So he stood still and took in everything about her.

Her long dark hair was loose and free, framing her lovely face. Her legs were, once again, sexy-long in black leggings and, so far, one thigh-high boot.

The rest of her outfit was black lace. A very short tunic-dress affair, heaven help him. Demure in coverage, sexy in outline, and slashed at the front from neck to hem with an oversized orange zipper.

Classy, edgy, individual. Very Kitty.

He'd never met a woman like her. The meltingly pretty face and soft heart of the proverbial girl next door. The sexy chic of a fashion model. All the more alluring because she seemed totally oblivious to it herself. And the hint of mystery, of a self-confidence built the hard way.

She hopped on her one-booted foot and opened the door wider for him to enter. Motioning for him to sit in the only chair, she plopped herself down on the edge of the bed to zip up the second boot.

"What are you doing here, Rosco?" Her tone was mild, but he caught the irritation of being disturbed.

"Watching you dress, apparently." Surely she should have been ready by now. Pretending he wasn't in the hotel room of a sexy woman seemed pointless. "Where's your wedding outfit?"

"Waiting for the wedding." she said with exaggerated patience, swinging the long fall of her hair away from her face and smoothing the length of it with her fingers. "I've ripped one of the skirt buttons. I'll fix it before we leave."

Was she carefree about everything? "Details and timing, Kitty. You need to take more care."

"Nonsense. It's nothing." She smoothed her hair again, annoyance in every stroke. "Why are you really here?"

"To take you to brunch," he said. "For our last planning meeting." No point giving her a choice and the opportunity to say no.

"Things getting too hot for you at campaign headquarters?" She quirked an eyebrow. "Little sister taking charge of her own day, huh?"

He shifted uncomfortably on the ridiculously low chair, stretching his right leg out in front of him, and feeling an unaccustomed height disadvantage.

He'd definitely lost leverage with his sister, too, but he wasn't going to admit to that.

"Titania's arrived and sent Aunt Ethel into overdrive." That was as much as he was prepared to say about that debacle. "My time is better spent working with you. And you're a much more attractive alternative to Aunt Ethel." He grinned to ensure she knew he was teasing.

"Really," she said with an obvious bite as she crossed those long booted legs beside him. "But not nearly as attractive as Titania, I seem to recall from our first meeting."

Ouch. He should have stayed away from personal comments. "She looks like a Barbie doll who's had a recent accident with marker pens. I prefer someone more real."

Kitty gave a grudging little half smile, and he knew it was time to shut up. Kitty was gorgeous. If she didn't know it, he certainly wasn't going to risk a sexist label by telling her.

"Anyway, my wedding organizing is done," he continued, rubbing his hands together in what he hoped looked like relaxed satisfaction. "Everyone is where they should be. Cars ordered to deliver them to the wedding when they should be. So I'm a free man, and I want to eat."

"Well, you'll have to do it without me." She stood and moved across the small room with that slinky sway of hers.

He watched her stretch for her ever-present camera bag. "*My* work hasn't started yet," she said.

"That's why I'm here. To super…" He sensed her stiffen and checked himself. "To *support* you." He stood to regain some advantage. This wasn't going at all to plan. "You're right. I needed to escape the endless girl-talk," he said.

"More Aunt Ethels arriving soon?" She sounded genuinely sympathetic, although her laughing eyes held very female mockery.

"I'm at their mercy," he confirmed. "Can't spoil the wedding by talking back to them."

"No. That must be difficult for you," she agreed. "You'll have to grind your teeth and pay the dentist bill later, Rosco."

"I'd rather grind them over a good steak."

"You're like a dog with a bone." She chuckled, shouldering

her camera bag. "You should watch that. It's only attractive if you have furry legs and a cute tail."

She raised an eyebrow and pretended to study him carefully. "Hmm, maybe you fulfill half of the criteria."

"You think my legs might be furry?"

"Hard to say. Never seen them out of big-city trousers."

"I'm a big-city boy." They were flirting. He didn't want to. But it felt good.

She wagged a playful finger at him. "Who is eating alone."

"Okay, okay. I get it. No big meals before work."

She sighed and nodded. "I'm supposed to meet you at the house in two hours. I planned to chill out with the camera for an hour or so first."

"All right. If that's what you prefer." He worked to ignore a nonsensical feeling of rejection. "But I'll pick you up in an hour and take you to the house and then the church. As agreed, I need you to watch my bachelor back."

There's truth for you, he thought and shrugged the enormity of it off with a purposely self-deprecating grin. "I'm wedding phobic, Kitty."

She sucked her bottom lip and considered his face. "Me, too," she finally conceded. "However some reciprocal deal will be needed to secure my full support." She winked and his entire body rose to her teasing tone.

"Anything," he said. "I'm desperate."

"Just the way I want you." She laughed. "I have a completed photography project. It needs the love of a good publisher."

She was fun, but he wasn't guaranteeing anything. He had no plans for their relationship to continue after the wedding.

However, her enthusiasm continued to seduce him. "I have several good editors on staff who can review any future submissions," he relented. It couldn't do any harm, and he did feel a little guilty about dragging her into all the media innuendo.

"I want you to review it personally. It's a book of photographs of Bedouin life, very close to my heart, and it deserves to be assessed by you. I'm desperate," she joked, mimicking his earlier tone. "I need you to see me as something more than a wedding rookie."

He laughed, as she no doubt intended. "You talked me into it." He held his hands up in surrender. "I'll consider it." The one Bedouin shot he had seen was excellent. He'd give it a few moments of attention and some feedback; he wasn't committing to anything beyond that.

"Excellent. I'll pitch it to you after the wedding." Her huge brown eyes sparkled at him as she reached out her hand to shake his.

He took her hand in his, and the electricity between them twanged into a life of its own. He reveled in the sensual pleasure of it for a moment, then broke the contact before all business sense was lost.

• • •

When Kitty's precious alone time was up, she repaired the button and shimmied into the soft silken lining of her new black suit, slipping it easily over her lace tunic and boots. She had no intention of wearing the constricting skirt for any longer than necessary, whatever Rosco might think. Then she walked through the inn to meet him in the carpark.

"Work hat on," she told him, miming a cone above her head as he picked up her heavy bag.

"I don't want to hear about bridesmaids, aunts, sisters, or the state of your dentistry while I work." *And no touching*, she thought, buckling in her seatbelt and leaning resolutely toward the door of his gleaming black SUV. When he left her an hour ago she'd had to shake the tingles out of her arm left by his mere handshake.

He stayed obediently quiet as the car purred along the short ride to the house just on the edge of the village.

"No paparazzi anywhere?" she asked. "I expected you to pick me up wearing a false beard and your gardening clothes." Not that she could imagine him as anything but immaculately dressed.

"Not a camera in sight," he confirmed. "All the security is in place and our combined subterfuge seems to have worked. We can relax."

Easy for him to say. For her, the serious work was just beginning.

The house was a generous two-story stone home with a huge garden that looked as if it had once been the gatehouse to the much larger manor just visible through trees.

Rosco opened the door into a stylish and classically modern décor of coffee and cream along with plenty of evidence of wedding chaos. Suitcases, garment bags, piles of presents, a dining room table covered in intricate floral arrangements.

Traditional cream and white with a dash of sparkle seemed to be the theme.

"Strength," she muttered to him as they inhaled hairspray and perfume.

"What a smell," he whispered, appearing to realize the words were heresy on this occasion.

Kitty silently agreed. She didn't do much girly stuff aside from lipstick and mascara, and after years of traveling and working in all climates, she really didn't care if that got forgotten along the way.

Her youngest sister, though, would love all this. The drama. The illusion.

"Upstairs, Kitty," called Amanda. "Only you. Not Rosco."

"Lucky," mouthed Kitty, as Rosco willingly walked away

to change into his wedding suit.

Kitty hefted her camera gear and went upstairs to apply herself to her art of illusion.

There was little needed beyond basic light control. Amanda was gorgeous and glowing in all cream and white, satin and lace. Her hair caught to one side, low on her neck in a loose braid, entwined with tiny white flowers and a sprinkle of sparkle to catch the light. The dress was a breathtaking triumph of couture design, both demure and sexy.

Rosco would hate it.

Excitement ebbed and flowed as the bridesmaids, sleek in the palest of pinks, joked and preened and posed.

Cara controlled her fidgeting on command, a little ballerina in two-tone pink with her basket of roses.

Titania fit right in, discreetly made up and asking for no special attention. Kitty smiled, contrasting this refined styling with the gaudy gold and purple image she had filtered into the tabloids.

Within an hour, every possible photographic angle had been covered with all of the females in the wedding party. And Kitty was sent away again to ensure Rosco left the house long before Amanda did.

Rosco was waiting for Kitty at the bottom of the stairs, ready for his next duty, crisp and handsome in a black suit and white shirt.

She paused on the landing, pretending to check her camera lens cap, while she took control of the sudden wobbles in her stomach and willed her fingers to stop shaking.

He was totally hot. Too hot.

"Just a few more hours of suffering for you," she whispered to him when she reached the last step. "Get me to the church."

"The sooner the better," he muttered. Grouchy Rosco was back.

Yet at the ceremony, she watched him treat his sister with infinite care and pride as he walked her slowly down the church aisle, past the polished wooden pews, to the simple altar steps.

Rosco remained subdued during the outdoor photo shoot but didn't interfere, and whenever needed, he was her considerate assistant. He drove her back to the inn, hours later in courteous silence.

Kitty, missing his earlier banter, reminded herself that this was the professional relationship she had asked for.

A wall of chatter hit them as they walked into the reception venue. She was swept along with him on a tide of Irish accents as his father's family surrounded him.

"As I was saying earlier, Rosco, you look just like your father."

"Yes, Aunt Kathleen. So you did," murmured Rosco.

Kitty was pinned behind his back by the drink-carrying crowd and couldn't see his face, but his tone was dangerously polite.

"You've got quite a job to do to live up to him. He would have given his girl a wonderful wedding party."

Kitty felt his spine stiffen, his whole body had that soldier-on-guard demeanor Ethel had triggered.

Mention of his father certainly tested his social skills. Kitty knew how that felt. Any mention of her mother had the same effect on her. She found negative memories were hard work and best exorcised in private.

But Rosco didn't retreat. The quality of his control seemed to intensify as he took a silent, steadying breath and reached out to pat his aunt's arm. "Yes," he agreed, none of his tension obvious in his voice. "And mother would have done the same."

Patience and respect overlaid his words, but Kitty noticed he didn't mention his father. "We must all work together to give Amanda the wedding she deserves," he continued, looking around the room for his sister. "Amanda looks like you, Aunt Kathleen. Mother always said she has your eyes."

"Her father's eyes," she agreed. "He was larger than life when we were growing up. Such fun." She sighed and dabbed her tears. "Big shoes for you to fill, lad."

Kitty caught the weight of expectation and a hint of judgment in her words, and she felt Rosco's patience fade. His body returned to combat mode and he still didn't mention his father.

She admired his restraint as he rode the waves of family concern and approval. It was an emotional whirlwind she wouldn't be able to navigate so smoothly herself.

As the crowd shifted, Kitty moved to Rosco's side. "Please excuse me," she said to his aunt. "I'm afraid I need to steal Rosco away from you for a moment."

She waved her camera by way of explanation. "He's in charge of the photography."

He turned with a well-mannered nod for his aunt and followed Kitty across the room to the glittery cream-and-white wedding party table.

"As promised, I've got your back," she said to him under her breath. She shoved the camera at him. "Here, pretend to look at this."

He did as he was told, and she turned to face him to ensure her words were only for him.

"I don't know what to say. Don't even know if I should say anything." What was work and what was personal now? She felt another uncomfortable little shift in her boundaries with this man and her motivation to impress him purely for business.

"Nice work," he said, still looking at the camera. "Keep

talking."

"We're comrades in arms," she said with a small amount of flirt to lighten the tone. "We live in different worlds, but family baggage dumping hurts anywhere."

She took a restless breath and lifted her hair up off her neck to cool down. "I recognize the tone even if I don't understand the details." She looked fiercely in his direction to find his blue-blue eyes looking straight at her.

"I've got your bachelor back. Let me know when you need me."

"Could be anytime soon." He winked, his Irish heritage, so much more noticeable in this family group, caressing his grim tone with a lilt of humor. Goose bumps again. The man made her cold all over. Then hot.

"Back to business. The best for Amanda," she said.

"That's the game plan." He nodded.

She took her camera from him, careful to avoid touching his hand with hers, and looped the strap around her neck. "Any last-minute advice for this round of photos?"

"Just keep to our agreed schedule."

The camera work leveled her emotions, drew her attention.

Dusk fell as the first dance was called, and she moved around the edge of the dance floor, lining up her penultimate volley of shots.

The bride and groom, Amanda and Rosco, Fiona and her husband. Then Cara and Rosco, her ballet slippers on top of his shoes, a giggling little marionette to his approximation of a slow waltz.

They earned a charmed round of applause, and then everyone was dancing and mingling. The bridesmaids danced with the groomsmen and the best man, with several other paraplegic friends, did a wheelchair bop as the music tempo rose.

Kitty lowered her camera and watched. Her work was nearly done, just the bouquet toss and honeymoon escape to go. She would tackle the proofing tomorrow. Weariness gnawed at her conflicted emotions. Weddings still weren't for her. And for some reason, tangled in her own family history, this wedding had become a little bit more than just a job. The layers of emotions around this one would be much less complicated if she didn't like these people.

They were all so lucky to have each other. Titania danced with each of the groomsmen in turn and appeared to thoroughly enjoy not being the center of attention. Kitty knew the pop star was planning to leave early in a dark-windowed car waiting at the back entrance. She would be gone before the bride and groom, leaving all of the limelight for them.

• • •

Across the room, Rosco picked Cara up, took her to her mother, then mingled with the guests. The man was an enigma.

His aunts, Kathleen and Ethel, with wine-flushed cheeks, had joined forces, and they intercepted their nephew with purposeful, handbag-holding strides.

He stopped in his tracks, taut with tension, and Kitty moved swiftly toward him. This was the dangerous social mingling time for Rosco. Time for her to deliver on her promise.

She wanted to laugh.

The aunts would make a great comedy duo. Kathleen with her iron-gray hair pulled into a tight bun, and Ethel with her helmet of lacquered waves.

"We want a talk with you, Rosco," Kathleen said seriously as Kitty hovered behind him, setting up imaginary camera shots.

"You should be married by now," said Ethel, folding her

arms. "Whatever's the matter with you, lad?"

"Your father isn't here to get you settled, and he'd want us to look after you," continued Kathleen.

"So we have a plan," said Ethel, adjusting her handbag firmly. "A plan to find you a wife, since you can't manage it for yourself. We want to see you dancing with Titania. Many a romance started with a bridesmaid at a wedding, you know."

"She's perfect for you, lad." Kathleen stepped closer to her nephew. "Your parents would have loved her."

"Yes." Ethel touched Rosco's arm. "Your father would have thoroughly approved of her spirit."

"She knows how to party. Just what you need. You're far too serious for your age," Kathleen continued. "Your mother would want us to steer you in the right direction."

They were crowding Rosco, piling on the family guilt, and Kitty bristled again on his behalf. But Rosco, smooth as Irish malt, took charge of his own destiny. "To be sure, that's grand of you, Aunties," he said. "Why don't you sit at that free table across the dance floor and I'll bring you some tea and cake."

He set them on their way toward the table and turned toward the refreshments.

Kitty was waiting for him. The man needed her in rescue mode again. It was time to step up the pretend photography supervisor ruse.

"Bleep, bleep, bleep," she said in his ear, her tone at full flirt volume. "Forget the cake. Count to ten and then follow me. Second door on the right."

Chapter Seven

Rosco opened the door into the soft, dusky darkness of a small function room.

"Kitty?"

"Don't turn the light on."

"Where are you?" His eyes were becoming accustomed to the gloom, but he couldn't see her anywhere.

"I'm under the far table, in the corner, by the wall. The one with the white tablecloth."

"Whatever for?"

"Because Ethel will be following you." Kitty's high heel waved at him from the floor. "Hurry up, Rosco."

"Ethel isn't on roller skates," he said, bending over and sticking his head under the tablecloth. "She'll still be waiting patiently for her tea, putting the world to rights with Kathleen."

"She's a handbag-toting Dalek. And she's got you locked in her sights." She stuck her arms out in front of her and swiveled them rigidly. "Matrimony. Matrimony."

He grimaced. "Ethel doesn't scare me. I'm never getting

married."

"Neither am I. So you'll be safe under here." She wriggled over into the corner to make room for him.

"*Rosco?*" They both heard Ethel's imperious tone calling down the short corridor.

"Women," he muttered, tossing up between two ridiculous options. He went for the funny, sexy one.

"Have you closed the door?" hissed Kitty as he folded himself into her makeshift tent.

"Yes," he hissed back. "Do you think I wanted anyone to see me talking to a stiletto heel under a table?"

"Smart thinking," she said, her brown eyes shining with irresistible pleasure at their absurdity.

They listened, silent for a moment, but there were no more calls from Ethel.

"I think we've bought some time," Kitty whispered. "But she'll be back. So keep your voice down."

He sat on one of the small dining-chair cushions and squashed another one into the small of his back as he leaned against the wall.

This was beyond absurd. And worst of all, his right leg ached from the dancing. He cursed the childhood memories it stirred as he eased his knee into a slightly more flexed position.

"Here," said Kitty, shoving another cushion at him. "Put this under your knee. I've noticed you massaging your leg. Is that a new injury?"

He arranged the cushion, buying some time. Everyone who needed to know about his leg already knew. It meant he didn't have to talk about it, and that's the way he wanted it.

"Old," he said, dismissing it along with memories of rehabilitation. "I was an adventurous kid."

He settled back, the ache lessening, and looked at Kitty. She was close, snuggled in her cushions, her knees now bent up under her chin, her ubiquitous camera bag at her feet.

The light floral perfume she favored was warm on her skin, and her lovely liquid-brown eyes assessed him with concern. He looked away. Maybe it was true, you really could drown in a woman's eyes. Good thing he was a strong swimmer.

"Where is your wedding outfit?" He realized she was barely covered again, wearing her short black lace dress and those damn thigh-high boots.

She gave him a sheepish little grin and patted a carefully folded pile of clothes tucked in beside her. "I've popped the button again. Three actually. All that bending and crouching to get the best photos."

She was teasing in that annoying way again. "You have trouble staying covered up, Kitty."

"Photography needs freedom of movement."

"I hadn't realized how physically demanding it is."

"Very," she assured him with a laugh. "You should be impressed I brought this back-up dress."

There was an element of touché in her tone, and he turned away from her, suppressing a sigh. There was no point in encouraging her by arguing, and it wouldn't do him any good for her to know how much that short skirt had caught his attention.

"You've furnished this well," he said, looking up at the rough-sawn underbelly of the old trestle table. "Cushions and wineglasses. Very comfortable." Not that he had a need for wineglasses.

"It's all I could find in here. Not too down market for you, Mr. Redmond?"

"It reminds me of when we were kids. Long summer holidays playing forts with Fiona and Amanda. Hardly an appropriate work venue." What had gotten into him, speaking of childhood memories with a virtual stranger…and employee.

"It's fun." Her voice held a hint of exasperation. "You should try and enjoy life. Your sisters missed out on the Irish accent, but they seem to have stolen your share of the fun factor."

"I don't need a fun factor." His father's alcohol-soaked grin swam into his memories. "My sisters need me to run the family businesses. That's my kind of fun."

"You need a balance. You're so left brain."

"What rubbish. I can't believe I'm under a table, talking about brain power." She'd taken this escape from his aunts to an absurd extreme. Way outside his comfort zone, even with the cushions.

"You're all logic and properness. No wonder your right leg aches—your left brain must be so big your right leg has to share the extra weight."

"That's doubly ridiculous." She was laughing at him, and it would feel so good to join in. When had he become afraid to laugh?

"Your sisters would understand."

"They've been double trouble as long as I can remember." He pulled his body as far away from Kitty as he could. "It's my job to be the responsible one."

He risked a glance at Kitty's face. Her brown eyes continued to shine with her unique spark of amusement. This wasn't going at all the way he wanted it to. It was supposed to be work, with him in charge.

"What about you?" He needed some balance here. She was witnessing his private family moments, and he knew nothing of her life. He wasn't interested *personally*, it was merely prudent to know an employee's circumstances and to stop talking about his own. "You know all about my family. Time I learned something about yours."

"Not much to tell." She did a little stationary jig with her heels and hugged her booted legs. "It's all a bit…

unconventional."

"You do surprise me."

Suddenly, into the dusky quiet, a rock anthem belted out from her bag.

"Oh no. Excuse me." She scrambled her hand around inside her bag.

"Hi," she whispered into a white cell phone splashed red and blue with a Union Jack. She nodded, twisted, and looked covertly in his direction. "No. I'm fine."

She listened some more. Nodded intently, and looked straight at him. "We're trending across all social media."

His gut tightened. The last thing he needed. "How bad is it?"

Kitty listened again as a slow smile spread across her anxious mouth. "Could be worse," she told him. "We're attached to hashtag bridesmaidtitania. No new pics of us."

Relief coursed through him. All those years of careful management would count for nothing if this blew up.

He reached out, patted Kitty's arm as she listened again to her caller. He recognized the tension in her face, in her tight grip on her phone. She hated this, too.

"No. No problem," she said softly into her phone, biting her lip. "Sorry, I lost track of time." Another pause. "No, I don't need rescuing."

She grinned into the phone, her usual up-beat humor returning. How he'd grown, in such a short time, to appreciate that warmth.

"Thanks for checking up on me," she joked, but he read true affection.

"A boyfriend?" he couldn't resist asking after she ended the call. Not that he cared, of course.

"No." She shook her head. "My sisters. Wondering if I needed rescuing."

"From me?"

"Big head. They don't know you." She pretend-punched his arm.

"Obviously not if they think you're at risk with me." If anyone was at risk of anything, it was him. He'd never allowed a woman to lure him under a table before. He pretend-rubbed the spot she had pretend-punched.

"How many sisters do you have?"

"Four."

"Well, let's start with them."

"Okay. But I'll pour some wine first," she said, obviously stalling for time.

He watched her surreptitiously as she rummaged in her bag, acutely aware of the leather of her boot brushing against his trouser in the confined space.

She produced a small screw-top bottle of red wine and poured herself half a glass.

"How much?" She gestured at the second glass.

He shook his head. "I don't drink. And I've just eaten a wedding feast." He undid his jacket button at the thought of it. "I won't need any food or drink for a week."

"Well, excuse me. I'm hungry now."

"You didn't have to be. Food was ordered for you." She looked delicious herself. Where did that thought come from?

"I didn't want it then."

"I remember, you're anti-food when working."

"Quite right, boss." She rummaged through her bag again and produced a muesli bar. "Mmmm, chocolate coated, perfect with red wine."

She settled back, food and drink in her hands. "A glass of wine relaxes me."

He could feel her reluctance to share and half of him regretted prying. Plus, he'd found alcohol-infused conversation distasteful for as long as could remember.

Yet she seemed vulnerable when she mentioned her

personal life, her past. He knew all about that, and his heart stuttered to know she also suffered from childhood wounds.

She sipped and sighed with pleasure, reaching out to waggle her fingers in his face. It was a reassuring connection just as he had felt compelled to offer when she was on the phone. But it was also flirty. An unconscious Kitty flirt all wrapped up in boots and lace and acres of creamy skin. "I'll think about the best plan for Ethel when I've finished the wine."

"Let me worry about my family," he said, unable to stop looking at her. He'd brave her sexy magnetism to ensure he could read the truth in her eyes. She was so close, and he'd never felt so tempted to touch. To soothe. To just let go. "You were going to tell me about *your* family."

• • •

Kitty avoided his gaze and tried to tune out his deep, honeyed brogue. She nibbled on her oat bar, sipped a little wine, procrastinated as long as she could.

"I don't have a family." The sooner she drank all the wine, the sooner she would find all this a little easier.

"Four sisters aren't family?"

"Half sisters." She nibbled and sipped again.

Rosco was watching her, those blue eyes star-bright in their gloomy hiding place. She suddenly worried about crumbs on her mouth, chocolate on her chin.

He had a five o'clock shadow developing on his strong jaw, and he rubbed his hand across it as he watched her.

"Blended families aren't unusual," he said. "I'd still call them a family."

"Not mine." She gave up on the muesli bar and concentrated on the wine.

"We've settled on 'the Sisterhood.'" She drained the glass

and felt the wine finally begin to untangle the knots inside her. Two days of happily-ever-after was probably two days too many for her. Perfect for Amanda and Andrew, but not part of her world.

"We all have different mothers." She'd stick to the facts. He didn't need to know too much. "I have three older sisters. They're all tall, and like me, look a bit like our father. And one younger sister." She smiled, hoping that was enough.

"Busy time for your father." Dry. Dry as a bone.

Kitty grinned. "We're all close in age, so yeah, I guess he had a good time for a few years."

"Not very prudent," he said, tight-lipped suddenly.

"Probably why we're all single and focused on work. We all run our businesses out of shared premises." She wasn't losing professional ground with him. "I'm not my father's daughter in the life choices department."

"I fully understand that," he said, in a tone that made her believe he really did.

"Good. So does that satisfy your curiosity?" she asked, her face still so close to his.

"No." He leaned forward, almost touching her, his finger pointing at her face. "Muesli. On your chin." His eyes stayed on the spot as she located the crumb. Her chin tingled from his gaze, almost as if he'd touched her. In fact, she could have sworn he'd wanted to. She rubbed out the tingle, avoiding catching his eye. "Sorry. There goes my ladylike status. My sisters say I'm the messiest. But my youngest sister is worse. We call her Little Litter Bug. And Bug for short, because she is. She's nothing like our father."

"What's your nickname?" His mouth twisted into a teasing smile and looked five years younger, his face the most relaxed she'd seen it.

Even a real smile wasn't going to coax that out of her. "Not telling you. I want you to think of me as a pure professional."

"Too late, Kitty. We're hiding under a table, and it wasn't my idea. Tell me," he repeated, his voice extra soft, implying her secret would be safe with him.

She took a breath, considering the fallout. She really wanted those future contracts with his company. But she couldn't be someone she wasn't, either. Not for long. "Jabbering Gerbera."

He laughed, head back, shaking silently, then returned his attention to her face. "Perfect," he said into the sudden quiet and caressed her face with his eyes, a soft, sexy blue gaze. "You're a gerbera girl?"

Kitty swallowed, nodded, took command of her speech. "Favorite flower." Always had been. At first it was to spite her mother. Or, at least, to stake a claim for individual identity. "Jacqueline, my mother, always wanted expensive, hothouse flowers. In huge extravagant displays." And paid for by rich men.

Kitty had known forever that she was nothing like her mother.

"Gerbera's are cheap and cheerful," she said. "And tough."

"Strong-stemmed," agreed Rosco. "Pretty and bright." His eyes crinkled appreciatively at her, and again she felt as if he had touched her. As if he wanted to. "Do you photograph them? They aren't on your websites."

"Yes, and no."

"So…?"

"I work with a graphic designer on my commercial art. It doesn't quite fit our other business profiles." She hugged her booted legs, happy at the thought of the last eighteen months of business growth.

"The gerberas are our signature. We don't have our names on the Jabbering website; we've tried a whole new approach. Our clients live on social media, and that's where we sell our look. Funky. Fun. Lots of white background and splashes of color."

"Just social media?"

"Plus email inbox drops. Abbey, my partner, uses a cool email tool to round out our publicity. Jabbering Gerbera has a cartoon logo, Gerbera Girl, who looks, ahem…a little like me."

"Let me guess. High heels and big Betty Boop eyes."

"And a huge orange camera," she confirmed.

"You get plenty of work that way?"

"As much as we can handle. We don't even need to share office space. All the work is online."

He nodded several times, considering her words. "Your own website is darker, edgy. Moody, I'd say. Nothing like you."

She wagged a finger at him. "You hardly know me." Her history was a whole lot more complicated than she was willing to dredge up now. As soon as she had the Ethel fake romance thing sorted she'd be back to her own life.

"That can be remedied," he said. She looked at him, pondering. He filled their under-table space so powerfully with his wedding-suited crispness. He had her hormones on permanent simmer.

"I'm a workaholic, Supervision Man." They were flirting again, best acknowledge it, even though it wasn't going anywhere real.

"You already know heritage is my first love."

"It shows," he said. "Quality work needs passion and talent. You have them both."

Businessman Rosco was the one she wanted to work with. Enough to face her childhood memories in order to keep this contract and create an opportunity to pitch her Bedouin project.

"You promised you'd consider evaluating my project if I covered your back." Now was the moment to make it happen.

Might never come again.

She straightened her shoulders, trying for professional, sitting on a scratched wooden floor beneath a long white table cloth.

"This isn't the time or place." He looked up again, with a wry grin, at the grubby underside of the table.

"I have a proposal nearly ready to go," she persisted. Just because they were having some fun playing decoy didn't mean he could dismiss her professionalism. "I'll email you."

"No. I'd prefer a verbal presentation," he said. "That shouldn't be a problem for you."

"You're not taking me seriously. I hope this doesn't mean you won't follow through."

He rubbed his jaw again, all man-in-control. "I'll call you." He smiled, tapping his mouth with his fingers in restrained amusement. What a mouth. So close. All juicy plump on the manly planes of his face.

Silence fell between them as she mused on her life with her sisters and the two-day-old impact of Rosco's charismatic power. All new and already a complicated part of her future.

"Rosco, are you in here?" called Ethel invading their sanctuary as she opened the door and turned on the light.

Kitty put her finger to her lips, willing him with a warning glance to keep quiet.

She checked their feet. Both pairs were safely inside the boundaries of their tent.

"What a funny little room," Ethel's voice boomed in the emptiness. "It smells of wine, don't you think, Kathleen?"

"Yes, it does. A good red was James's favorite," said Kathleen in her softer voice, with its musical Irish lilt.

"I've missed him today. Been remembering growing up, the parties, the laughter. He could have married anyone, you know. Lydia was a lucky girl."

Rosco stiffened beside Kitty. Threateningly still.

Ethel's unmistakable harrumph followed. She walked toward their table, her solid black court shoes peeping under the tablecloth, dangerously close to Rosco's leg.

"I think I'll take a couple of these cushions back with us. Those chairs are so uncomfortable," she said. The table shook and the tablecloth swung as she rummaged above them.

"I thought Rosco would have been looking after us by now. He certainly hasn't inherited his father's social skills."

"I think that's a bit harsh, Ethel."

"He left us waiting for tea. And there's no sign of him looking after that lovely photographer. They implied they were a secret couple, but I've seen no evidence of it today."

She spun on her sensible heel and her foot was lost from view. Kitty let out a slow, silent breath.

"Makes me wonder if there isn't something the matter with him," Ethel continued, confiding and grumpy. "You know a confirmed bachelor. Past the point of no return. Stuck in his ways."

Her heels stumped across the wooden floor. "When I find him, I'll get him into Titania's arms. He's a lost cause without us."

Kitty put a restraining hand on Rosco's arm. Sitting still was now a noticeable challenge.

"Come along, Kathleen. We'll get our own tea."

The door closed behind them, and Rosco huffed out an exasperated breath.

Kitty buried her face in her knees, unable to stop her shoulders shaking.

"Stop laughing."

"*You*, past the point of no return. *You* stuck in your ways." She gasped, hiding her laughter behind her curtain of hair. "Not blessed with self-awareness, your Aunt Ethel, is she?"

Kitty twisted her head to look at him and stopped smiling. His face was livid, hard, and she so wanted to soothe the anger in his clenched jaw.

"Interfering old trout," he said, visibly releasing some anger with the words.

"Thanks very much. That's a long way from my aforementioned baby-faced, mushy-food-eating shortcomings."

He gave the weakest of smiles. She considered it a success and sighed, worried at the hurt in his face.

"My mother *wasn't* a lucky girl, not at all." His voice was flat, his eyes chipped ice.

Kitty's heart twisted. His mother had been hurt in this happy-looking family. *Appearances*, she thought. So often not what they seemed. She'd learned that long ago; it was mother's milk stuff to her. But each new disillusionment still upset her.

She waited, giving him time to deal with whatever was on his mind. He might be an exasperating controller—type A, if ever there was one—but the humor and affection for his family were also real.

He snatched the cushion under his right knee, thumped it on the floor beside him, plumped it viciously with both hands, and rammed it back under his knee.

"Life and soul of the party…" He fisted his hands on his knees. "My father's alcoholism wasn't pretty. When the party's over, alcohol isn't so lively."

Kitty knew that only too well. He was talking to her. Letting the professional mask slip, and she felt his pain. She placed her hand over his fist, the hard warmth of it increasing her awareness of his body next to hers. A sexy tug of attraction shot between them, and her breath caught as her own memories mixed with his.

"I was sixteen when my mother died," she said.

Rosco opened his hand beneath hers. "I was fourteen when my father died."

Kitty interlaced her fingers with his, curled them together

in unspoken support. His touch, firm and strong, gave her goose bumps and continued to arouse desires she didn't dare explore.

• • •

Rosco absorbed the calming comfort of Kitty's soft touch. Gratitude for her laughter and understanding mingled with pain and respect for the sixteen-year-old girl who had lost her mother. He would have hated that pain for his sisters at such a young age.

He looked at her, seeing the hurt, lonely child in the depths of her warm brown eyes. The brave girl now so grownup and sexy as she smothered her laughter in this absurd little hiding place.

Her shimmer and sparkle continued to pull him in. Away from memories. Away from business caution. Into temptation.

For once he wanted to give in to that temptation. For pleasure to win. He'd never again have the total privacy of Kitty's tablecloth hideaway.

Her body was tantilizingly close, beautiful and soft, warm and fragrant with her flowery perfume. He drank her in, and she didn't flinch from him as he moved his mouth closer to hers.

Refusing to analyze further, he hooked his finger gently under her chin and touched his nose to hers, asking silent permission to kiss.

He couldn't resist her unique blend of attraction. Fragile when she thought he wasn't watching, strong when rising to a challenge. Always sexy.

Kitty briefly held his gaze, and he could see she was grappling with her own blend of caution and attraction. Then she closed her eyes, tipped up her head, accepting his touch.

Desire pulled his lips to hers, his first kiss a gossamer

graze, caressing, still questioning, as he felt her mouth tremble beneath him.

He moved with infinite care to tease the pout of her bottom lip with his own, to taste, to explore.

Then her mouth melted with his, and nothing existed but her. He deepened the kiss, pulled back to graze, then deepened it again, ever so slowly, stoking the flames licking between his body and hers.

She returned the heat, and his gut twisted as she gripped the lapels of his jacket. He reveled in her touch, the softness, the tender responsiveness that went on and on.

Finally, when his control threatened to desert him, he broke the kiss. Pulling apart was a wrench, a full-body warning to cool it. The small part of his brain still thinking clearly recognized Kitty as a unique threat to his usual restraint.

He had to shut that down. She was an employee and still a mystery to him. He may have drawn her into her decoy role, but it wasn't viable in reality.

He caressed Kitty's cheek to lessen any rejection and kept his gaze on her mouth. She kissed as well as she talked, and he needed her to fill the sudden silence between them. To talk him down.

• • •

Kitty licked her lips, Rosco's kiss still trembling through her as they sat not touching. Not speaking.

Her cheek tingled from his last tender touch, and the pressure to kiss again built, threatening, as she fought to dredge up some humor.

"No one ever consoled me like that in grief sessions, Mr. Redmond." She bumped his shoulder with hers and felt him relax a little.

"I should hope not. Completely unethical." His gaze met

hers, and he laughed with a hint of shy warmth that confirmed he had enjoyed the kiss as much as she had.

"This makes us blood brothers, Redmond. What happens under the tablecloth, stays under the tablecloth." Her turn to laugh. "Oath?"

"Oath." He raised his right hand to his heart. "But no actual blood. This suit is new."

"Spoilsport."

He shrugged in pretend regret. "My aunts would be very suspicious."

"Ethel would take to you with a lecture and a washcloth."

"Aye. She would," he agreed with a grin, as Kitty's resolve to outwit Ethel doused the last of her heated hormones.

"I've seen the way you care for your family, and I admire it. But Ethel has no business judging you. Interfering in your life."

She bristled with indignation at the injustice. Ready to do battle on his behalf.

"Down, Gerbera Girl," he said. "I can keep my cool with Ethel for all-around family well-being." He grimaced in the dusky light. "I'm not saying it's always easy. But family business wasn't an obligation I expected of you when we signed our contract."

"I don't know how to be part of a family. So yours is quite safe from me."

"Let's not get hung up on the 'family' word again. You have a family, your sisters."

"Not like any you know."

"They phoned you. They care."

"Yes. We care. But we're making it up as we go along." She sighed and shifted against her cushions.

Might as well keep talking. They needed to fill in more Titania-avoiding time, and Rosco was right—she did know a lot about his family.

It was reasonable to share a little more after his huge leap of trust in revealing his father's alcoholism. She wouldn't betray that trust. But she wished it hadn't made him even more attractive. Too attractive to resist kissing.

But he'd have her checked out anyway, if he actually considered working with her on future projects.

"Two of my older sisters have always known each other. They went to the same boarding school. Their mothers were the only ones our father married, and they knew about each other but there was no rivalry. They were united in their eventual scorn for their shared husband."

"He paid for his daughters' education?"

"He did. And those two sisters have some memories of him occasionally arriving at boarding school, like Father Christmas, and taking them out to Sunday lunch, High Tea at the Ritz, or Harrods Food Hall."

"And what memories do you have?"

"None." She remembered asking her mother repeatedly about her father. "My mother said she was too young to settle down when I was born. She said she had insisted on an education fund for me. 'I didn't conceive you by myself,' she told me. I had to look the word conceive up in the dictionary. I thought babies were imagined for a while."

Rosco chuckled, and she liked the camaraderie with a hint of sensual appreciation now simmering between them. If she kept on talking, maybe this new non-business Rosco would stay around a bit longer. And see he could trust her.

"My other two sisters have the same story. An education fund but no father."

"So how did you all get together?"

"He had a stroke two years ago. Sent private detectives around the world to find us."

"Belated fatherly love?"

"Perhaps, a little." She shrugged. "He had businesses and

property. I don't think he wanted it broken up and given to his nephews."

She shrugged again. "I don't know if he loves people. The most I can say is he values education."

"And where in the world did he find you all?"

"London, Spain, and Paris times two."

"That's only four. Where were you, Kitty?"

"I was the hardest for him to find." She couldn't keep a certain pride from her voice. "And the hardest to get to dance to his tune." She remembered her anger at the intrusion into her life.

"A friend finally talked me into leaving Jordan. I'm used to living out of a rucksack, living simply in the history I'm recording. I had other plans after Jordan, and they weren't for London."

"So how long have you been here?"

"Eighteen months. I missed the first six months of the Sisterhood. I regret that now."

"And what has kept you here?"

She moved away from him, as far as she could. He, and the wine, were pulling her too far into herself now. Into feelings best left in the past.

She hugged her legs again, the best position in their cramped cave. "I always wanted a sister, and now"—she sighed happily—"I have four." Keep it in the present. Keep it light. Stick to the facts.

"*Two's* enough for me," he said. But they both knew he didn't mean it. "Five of you in one place," he teased. "How do the logistics of that all work out?"

"Ralph, our father,"—the word still felt alien to her—"has signed his property over to us. We all live and work together."

"Your father lives with you?"

"He lives in Spain, says he needs to follow the sun for his aching bones. It works." She wouldn't be around if he was living with them, that's for sure.

Rosco frowned at her, clearly confused. "You all live and work together in London?"

"Yes." She was enjoying this. In control of a conversation with Rosco for once.

"In the house you grew up in? Too small surely." He looked at her with sudden suspicion. "Are you in financial trouble, trying to support a new lifestyle with your sisters?"

She shook her head. "We live in a warehouse restoration on the *wrong* side of London," she said, comparing it to the prime real estate his family owned, in London and in Wheatbridge Village. "We're tucked into an industrial corner of the Thames. Part of a renewal community—a little urban village growing in the shadow of the city."

"Sounds expensive," he said, suddenly cool. "If you're trying to suck me into overpaying an advance on a new assignment, you won't be successful. If I contract you for any projects requiring an investment from my publishing house, you'll be vetted thoroughly." He leaned into her, assertive and in control.

"My business proposal is solid." He was still so skeptical of her, not that she could blame him. The way the media had flocked to his home, eager to tear him down, proved he was vulnerable to being exploited.

But it hurt that he still distrusted her after all her support with the paps and his aunts. "I'll be ready for you," she said, remembering their sizzling kiss. "My father is Ralph Kingston."

Rosco narrowed his eyes, processing the name, and Kitty saw the moment he realized her identity.

"You're a Brick Square heiress."

"I am. And believe me, I know all about working hard to protect a legacy."

He was silent. And she needed to get moving before his

implied distrust of her ate away at her energy.

"Let's go," she said, annoyed that she had allowed him to goad her into talking about her father. It was a first for her to reveal his identity, especially as some sort of proof of self worth. She'd never dreamed of having to use her father's name to prove herself to anyone.

"Time to work on our pretend romance to protect your bachelor stud status and my working future with LJ Redmond Publishing. I'm holding you to that presentation promise." They still had an hour or so to go before this contract was completed, and she wasn't finished cementing her position yet. There needed to be a big reward for talking about her father.

She leaned toward Rosco. Straightened his already straight tie. As if it would dare look askew, even squashed under a table.

"I know all about being asset rich and the worry of being too cash poor to protect it, to develop it. About having a father whose reputation shadows you."

He nodded, a calculating glint in his eye.

"That's why I understand the Titania thing."

He nodded again, and she hated that she wanted—needed—him to believe she was on his side. That was what happened when she started talking about herself. She started to care. And she'd allowed him to kiss her. Enough. She was through with this cloistered hideaway.

"Just a little fake romancing to get the aunts off your back and we'll be done. Are you still up for it?" The answering glint in his eye now held just enough smolder to stir her desire.

"I am." He looked ruefully at the table above them and then back down to hold her gaze with his. "Your secrets are safe with me. My oath still stands. What happens under the tablecloth stays under the tablecloth, Kitty."

His Irish burr caressed her name as the air between them

heated and stilled again with the power of temptation.

But she clicked her fingers, defusing the moment. She wasn't messing up her plan with more contract-endangering kissing.

"Come on, let's dance," she said. "I've got a stop-Ethel-in-her-tracks plan."

"I don't dance."

"Of course you do. I've seen you."

Chapter Eight

Rosco gave in. Impossible not to.

"What suffering do you have in store for us?"

"You'll see," she said. "It's time to say good-bye to the tablecloth."

"Thank goodness." He pulled a face and stretched his legs. "There's no room for Ethel in here, too."

Laughing in spite of himself, he rolled out of their hiding place and watched Kitty's long booted legs follow him as she shuffled to the edge, pushed her bag and folded wedding suit out ahead of her, and wriggled out to join him.

She shimmied her hips at him. "Ethel needs to be convinced of your studly prowess if you want her to leave you alone."

The fun Kitty radiated melted some of his carefully controlled caution as, still tempted beyond his usual common sense, he watched her smooth her lacy dress over her hips.

She then fluffed her hair around her face and pulled the oversized orange zip at her neck down a little to reveal more cleavage than his already heated body considered comfortable.

Kissing her had been a mistake. He was way too aware of her body now, and she was an even more complicated mystery to him. Why would a Brick Square heiress be working for him as a low-ranking photographer and be playing pretend games with his family?

"What are you doing?"

"I'm dressing up for dancing, for romance. We need to be convincing." She grinned at him, eyes sparkling again.

"More like dressing down." His eyes were automatically drawn to her bra, hot orange against the creamy swell of her breasts. He couldn't turn away. Didn't want to, as the heat of that kiss remained undiscussed between them.

The kiss and unanswered questions about her identity were potential risks he'd deal with later. Right now, he just needed this farce with his family to be over.

"You know I'm serious when I take time to preen," Kitty joked. "Ethel should be shaking in her shoes."

A shared vision of Ethel's stout shoes peeping under their tablecloth had them grinning together like children with a naughty secret.

Kitty's sexy humor warmed him, and he suppressed another wave of desire.

"Sometimes less is more," he whispered. Reaching for her, careful not to touch her skin with his, he slowly raised the orange zip of her dress. Wrapping away temptation. "Let's not give poor old Aunt Ethel a heart attack."

He felt Kitty suck in a quick breath as she placed her hand to her chest where his had adjusted the zipper. "Very good, Mr. Redmond. No relatives will be harmed."

She moved her hands to grip his lapels, her smile twisting his gut every bit as seductively as her breasts. "But. You will be required to put some effort in. To actually dance."

"I'm not hot stuff on the dance floor." He clutched his

right leg in mock pain. "Nothing too complicated. No salsa for me."

"Just slow dancing," Kitty said, moving close to him. "Swaying and flexing. No pressure."

"Easy for you to say," he murmured as she put her hands on his shoulders.

She swayed, and he moved with her, until the need to control the dance spurred him on.

He pulled her toward him, body to body. "Is this what you had in mind?" He was only human. And this round of flirting was decoy business. Never to be repeated.

"Mmmm," she said, considering. "I think you need a little technical supervision."

He smiled into her shining eyes as their swaying stilled to match their breathing, his held suddenly, waiting for her next move. "Supervise away, Kitty."

She took his face in her hands. "Your aunt will expect some convincing passion," she breathed into his ear.

"A peck on the cheek." She demonstrated.

"An affectionate meeting of foreheads." He met her halfway.

"A playful kiss on the lips after a particularly romantic slow tune."

He took over. Couldn't resist as his mouth found hers and he kissed her again. Soft, experimental.

He felt her quiver against him as their lips clung just a bit longer than a practice for pretending required. Every fiber of his being focused on her lips—on the gentle pull of attraction.

"Kiss, kiss, kiss," said Cara's voice, and they both jumped and peeled apart to see a slightly bedraggled little ballerina in the doorway, trailing a nearly-empty flower basket.

She pursed her lips in an exaggerated pout and made several big smacking, smooching sounds. "Kiss, kiss, kiss," she chanted and ran from the room.

"Women," he breathed. "Nothing but trouble from birth."

He should have known he'd suffer for abandoning his usual caution. A private kiss was very different from a public display with a family inquisition to follow.

"Showtime." Kitty grinned.

He adjusted his tie, straightened his jacket, and offered her his arm.

"Relax," she said, looping her arm through his. "No one will guess you've just spent forty-five minutes under a table."

He led her out of the room into the short dim corridor but stopped before they opened the door to join the party.

He needed to know what he'd missed during his time with Kitty. "I have to check in with security," he said, hitting speed dial on his cell phone.

They answered immediately. "Update," he demanded.

Gratifyingly professional, they had the precise information he wanted to hear.

"Titania has left the party," he reported, pocketing his phone. "No trace of any media anywhere, and security is still in place until the bridal party leaves."

He felt her relax on his arm. Sometimes he sensed she was as uptight as he was, despite her bubbly humor and the lust for life that still tingled where his lips had kissed hers.

Questions about why she was so private nagged at him. It had to be more than who her father was. But he let relief at escaping any Titania-related gossip shots override his concern.

He couldn't afford Titania's reputation as a social hell-raiser to be attached to him personally or to the business. The Sandford Palace contractors were looking for scandal-free credibility.

Just this fake romantic dance with Kitty to get the aunts off his back and he'd be free. The last family wedding successfully negotiated. "Let's get this over with."

They joined the party arm in arm, and he scanned the

room, looking for his aunts.

"This way," he said, locating his family sitting in a group on the edge of the dance floor.

Cara pursed her lips at the sight of them, enjoying the sound of several huge smooching noises.

"My, what a wonderful goldfish you make, Cara," said Kitty, joining in with another round of lip pursing and smacking.

She removed her arm from his and bent down to Cara's level, dancing an impromptu swimming stroke with the rhythm of his niece's chanting.

"Aunt Ethel," he said, ensuring he had her attention for their performance. "Please look after Kitty's bag while we dance. They're playing my kind of music."

Kitty moved into his arms on cue, as soft and sexy as she looked, and he felt his worries recede and far more pleasurable tensions take over his body again.

She moved in close, humming quietly to the schmaltzy tune as she placed her hands on his shoulders.

Rosco couldn't help himself, he pulled her closer and touched his forehead to hers. "Nice move," she encouraged, winding her arms round his neck. "You're a good man," she murmured. Her mouth was right beside his ear, her breath warm and sweet. "You deserve to relax."

"You're not a relaxing woman." She might be at ease with her body, but she was all new to him.

"I'm not relaxed enough?" she asked, mischievous.

He groaned softly. "I should have kept my mouth shut."

She wriggled even closer, soft and pliant.

Rosco lost audio on the band.

All he could hear was the pounding of his own blood as she swayed against him.

Kitty stirred, nuzzling into his neck. "Hold me closer."

He drew her hips to his and she leaned in, tightening her

arms at his neck, linking her hands in his hair. He caressed the length of her elegant back, the lines long and smooth, then settled his hands on the soft lace fabric at her waist, spread his fingers over the small of her back.

They rocked gently, her fingers softly massaging the back of his neck, languorous, seductive. He closed his eyes and let time slip away.

Too soon the band upped the tempo to rock-pop and jerked him back to reality. He pulled quickly away, lessening their bond. His mind wanted to step completely away, but his hands still lingered at her waist.

"This music isn't for me," he said. Just as well, as he was finding the pleasure of her in his arms all too enticing.

"Just a little longer," Kitty said, placing her hands over his at her waist. "Ethel, Kathleen, and a man I presume is Kathleen's husband, are watching us. They look a little disapproving."

"Aye, that'd be right. There's no pleasing them."

"There you go, all Irish again. Music to my ears." She squeezed his hand. "Just one kiss, I think, to seal the deal."

He wouldn't go there. It was *too* tempting. Even as his body strained to do as she asked, the business caution he relied on overruled desire at last.

He risked a smile and a kiss to her cheek, then stepped away.

"That will have to do them." None of this was real.

He turned away from her, blocking out the temptation. "Thirsty work this acting. Let's find a cold drink."

• • •

Kitty followed him to the bar, working hard to clear her head.

He was right. She was thirsty, too, but the reason was him. He was hot.

That private under-table kiss had those now familiar Redmond-induced goose bumps fizzing all over her body. His plump, juicy mouth too gorgeous to resist.

It was just a kiss. But she'd never felt so cherished, even if it wasn't for real. The peck on the cheek while dancing was obviously the reality of their decoy game. "It's back to work for me," she said after a few minutes, leaving her empty glass with him. And time to leave their performance behind.

She had willingly agreed to this fake romance, it'd been mostly her idea, even. But their brief kiss was still imprinted on her lips, and it triggered feelings she'd never had before. Feelings totally at odds with her desire for a professional relationship with his publishing company. Feelings obviously not reciprocated when he'd given her a chaste peck on the cheek and practically abandoned her on the dance floor.

It was over now. She left him with a small forced smile and headed across the room toward Ethel.

"Thank you very much for looking after my bag," she said, sitting in one of the now vacant chairs beside Rosco's aunt.

"Glad to help, my dear," she said. "I'm pleased to see you dragged my nephew onto the dance floor. Damned cruel the way that leg holds him back." She scowled.

There was more to this leg injury than childhood adventure. Kitty looked around for Rosco but couldn't see him. Curiosity nipped at her, but she didn't want Ethel's version of the story. She wanted Rosco's.

"He could have been in one of those wheelchairs himself." Ethel sniffed, and Kitty heard genuine concern beneath the now familiar gruffness. "He's a fighter, I'll give him that." She shook her head and tutted out a long sigh. "You have a good heart, my dear," Ethel continued. "And you know how to wear a pair of heels—loved them myself years ago." She smiled warmly. "Enjoy them while you're young."

Kitty was moved. She leaned over and kissed Ethel's cheek. "Thank you." She smiled, raising her legs out in front of her and turning the boots from side to side to admire the heels.

"Young Rosco won't be able to resist them," Ethel advised quietly. She winked. "Worth fighting for, that one."

"You're distracting me from my work," Kitty admonished. "I've got flower tossing and honeymoon escaping to record."

She scrabbled around inside her camera bag, selected camera and lens, and began her usual checking and cleaning routine. Her mind, however, was busy elsewhere.

She wondered why Rosco wouldn't talk about his leg injury. Why he was lucky not to be in a wheelchair? "The wheelchair boys are going to line up in a guard of honor at the end," said Ethel.

"What's their connection to Andrew?" Kitty asked, realizing Ethel could be a mine of Redmond information.

"Andrew is a sports physician. He also plays with the wheelchair basketball team they all belong to."

"Andrew plays wheelchair sport?"

"Yes. Same as Rosco. Rosco is also Andrew's patient. He's always looking for the latest physiotherapy options."

"You sound very well informed, Ethel."

"The girls keep me up to date. We all worry about Rosco."

Kitty nodded, more information to process, more of Rosco to understand. She told herself her curiosity was because she wanted their business future to flourish.

And she hoped she hadn't jeopardized it with the sexy dancing and kissing. Their romance wasn't real—she needed to remember that.

Relief from her swirling thoughts arrived with the bride. Back to work.

"We're almost ready to leave, Kitty."

"Ethel just mentioned the guard of honor."

"Yes, we need to get on with that so the boys can get back to London in the team bus."

"Isn't the bouquet throwing next?" She'd memorized the rituals, hoping to hide her total lack of wedding experience.

Amanda nodded. "We'll use the band's microphone to thank everyone for coming and then I'll throw my bouquet from the stage."

"It's always such a fun thing," said Ethel. "I remember when your mother caught mine."

Amanda took her aunt's hand and held it gently. "We have the photos. It was a beautiful bouquet, and mom had exactly the same at her own wedding."

Family memories, age-old rituals which had never been part of my life, thought Kitty. She sighed as happy and sad mingled together.

She slipped away and got to work deciding on her best angles. She was ready when Amanda and Andrew finally arrived on stage. Their thanks were heartfelt, and their obvious belief in the wonderful future ahead of them was palpable. Kitty only hoped, for once, life lived up to expectations.

The bouquet was caught by one of the bridesmaids, but not without a spirited pretend attempt by one of the guys in a wheelchair to intercept it. He caused much laughter as he held up an empty hand in defeat, then zoomed back to his teammates to stand guard at the door.

Kitty sped after them to complete her last volley of shots. Some low work showcasing the lines of wheels had an edgy-art look of its own.

When Amanda and Andrew stopped to kiss between the lines of wheelchairs, the guys threw handfuls of rose petals into the air around them. It was a distinctive shot, soft flowers, metal wheelchairs, Amanda's beautiful back, and a whole lot of fun.

"Good luck," Kitty whispered as she took the last photo.

She stepped back, no longer part of the action, and let everyone surge past her as Amanda and Andrew ran for their car.

"Great work, Gerbera Girl," Rosco whispered in her ear.

Kitty smiled. "Thanks," she said with a burst of pleasure at his compliment and unexpected attention. "Where are they going now? I won't tell anyone."

"To Chopper House. It's about thirty minutes out of the village. I own it with two friends, and we've promised to leave them alone for a week."

"Chopper House?"

"Helicopter. The three of us own the chopper, too; we've got a landing pad and hangar cover."

"I guess that means you're staying at your mother's house with Ethel." She couldn't resist teasing him, especially now that she understood how much of a soft spot his aunt had for her courageous, complicated nephew.

Rosco pulled a face but didn't seem to be genuinely bothered.

"Do you live at Chopper House usually?"

"Not often enough. It's a sort of man-cave retreat for the three of us. Lots of chopper talk and steak eating."

Kitty shuddered, pretending to be horrified, but she was really delighted that he was talking so much about himself.

"So you live in the townhouse, with the gold and purple decorations?" She was too curious about him to listen to her inner caution.

"Yes." He smiled at their shared subterfuge. "The townhouse belongs to the family, and I live there most of the time."

Then a shout of laughter interrupted them, and they both rushed out as Amanda and Andrew prepared to drive away.

Suddenly it was all over.

Kitty's energy sagged as she watched most of the guests

slowly leave the wedding. Young women in party dresses, carrying their high heels, men with their suit jackets slung over one shoulder. Rosco's aunts wiping away tears as they cornered him for a final round of family photos on someone's cell phone.

Sadness filtered through her tiredness. She'd done her best, put her heart into her photography, given Rosco the bridesmaid saving diversion he needed, and now the three days that felt like a lifetime were over.

She craved the privacy of the drive back to London to think it all through before she processed her photographs and completed the wedding albums over the next few days.

But Rosco walked toward her through the thinning crowd, his cell phone to his ear, and held up his hand to stop her from leaving with the last of the guests.

His lips, so full and sexy just a short time ago, were now compressed in a serious straight line.

Alarm stopped her in her tracks. "What's wrong?"

He stabbed at his phone, disconnecting the call. "Security. A guest broke my no cell phone photography rule and posted an image of us dancing on Instagram."

She stiffened and clenched her hand around the strap of her camera. "You and me? Are there comments?"

He squinted at the screen. "Give me a minute to find it."

The man was prehistoric with technology. She couldn't endure his fumbling. "Give it to me." She grabbed the phone from him and thumbed her way to the image.

The comments, tabloid-like in their brevity and disregard for privacy, goaded her. She'd been too smug about getting away with their aunt-fooling stunt. "London tycoon dances the night away. Is he next for matrimony? Way to go, Rosco. Who is his mystery woman?"

Kitty shoved the phone back at him. "So much for my anonymity."

Rosco scanned the message with a grunt and stabbed his screen to cancel the image. "I'm happy with it. It's only a head shot. Could be worse if that short skirt of yours was on display." He raked a now familiar disapproving glance at her dress.

"It's only Instagram, not the news media, and your face is only partly visible." His own face hardened, contradicting his stated acceptance, and her heart sank.

"*You're* happy with it." The cheek. It was her privacy. Obviously for him it was just another strategic decoy shot.

"Yes. This is why you needed to keep your dress zipped. I said I couldn't guarantee the actions of others."

"You could sound more concerned. That dancing was for *your* family, for *your* benefit."

"I didn't ask for it." Anger evaporated all her pleasure in the wedding and the fun of their decoy ruse. "You seemed a very willing participant to me. It's just wedding madness. No one knows who you are." His arrogance was back in spades as he gave her another controlling stare.

"I may not be recognizable in the photo," she conceded. "But I'm not fine with it."

"It's over. Go home." He strode away as his phone rang again, leaving Kitty glaring after him with a few choice words left unsaid.

If only he were right. She snuck away to collect her things for the trip. The biggest prize she'd hoped to be taking back to London was her escape from the paparazzi.

Now that threat wasn't gone.

Chapter Nine

Rosco hit the motorway for London at dawn the next day.

All the nonsensical paparazzi rumor mongering had developed a surprising positive twist.

He'd checked his emails after the wedding to find an invitation to progress contract negotiations with the Duke of Sandford and Trinity St. George.

They confirmed LJ Redmond Publishing had moved on to the next step on the short list process—an interview at their palatial heritage home.

They particularly commented on Rosco's discretion in handling the media during his association with Titania. His consistently prudent public image impressed them, and they were delighted to see, following his photo prior to his sister's wedding, that he had a stable and suitably private personal life with his "mystery woman."

The final contenders for the contract would be listed on the Sandford website. The contest was to become a publicity event for the palace, a photo fest to attract visitors to the heritage site.

Rosco gripped the steering wheel and let his rented Bentley hum along the empty motorway. Publishing was a tough business, and this development didn't surprise him. He was up for the fight, and he felt a welcome wave of combative energy.

Reviewing the contract details carefully, he remained convinced his proposal would ultimately succeed. He had a team of photographers and writers who had developed the preliminary proposal and were ready to go on the final project.

The opportunity it provided to secure his mother's publishing legacy was the culmination of all he had worked for. Discreet. Sober. Vigilant.

The only downside was the irony that this attention from the duke ensured an increase in the very thing he loathed on a personal level. Ramped up media coverage.

A quick early morning search revealed there were already additional shots of the times he and Kitty had been ambushed at his townhouse. No fresh news. Just repetitive innuendo. And the now entrenched title for Kitty—his mystery woman.

She'd saved him twice from the Titania fallout. Once with the media and then again with his family. He owed her, and that debt burned deep. It was the kind of complication he'd always avoided. He'd been right about that for all these years, because now that he'd given in to the temptation of Kitty, his attraction to her was yet another problem he didn't need.

And now, thanks to the duke and his wife, he was trapped for a bit longer in this soap opera.

He needed to keep Kitty close to help seal his contract as his mystery woman. And that gumption and talent was worth keeping on his team. He didn't want her poached by any other publishing firm, especially now that she knew so much about his family.

He also wanted to protect her. There was bound to be more paparazzi coverage, rehashed photos, and insinuations.

He also needed to be sure of her continued discretion. He wanted to know as much about her as she did about him, and that had sparked an idea for an offer he hoped she couldn't refuse.

An offer to write the history of Brick Square would give him more time with her. Business was on his mind, but his body just wanted to dance with her again. It was the type of attraction to an employee that he had forbidden himself to ever allow, but he could control it.

Kitty's situation as his mystery woman was unique. He'd had no idea when he'd answered his front door to her boots and Christmas-colored woolens that he would be in her debt. Now her decoy role was a fixture in his life he needed to manage for a little longer.

Her Brick Square heritage was the perfect project to keep her close for purely business reasons.

He drove across the city, aiming for a late breakfast at Fuchsia and Lime.

Parking some distance away, he raised his jacket collar against a cool breeze and approached Brick Square from the Thames river path. The view across a large flag-stoned quadrangle gave him an uninterrupted appreciation of the south wing of the complex.

Its website had provided him with all the facts and figures. The complex covered one small city block. The south wing had been fully restored and offered two large business premises on the ground floor—the Fuchsia and Lime series of eateries and the Brick Square Child Care Center.

But the impact of the actual building was impressive, rustic and pretty with arches and turrets.

Walking toward it slowly, he appreciated the scale, understood the passion he'd seen in Kitty's eyes for this urban village emerging out of the industrial fringe of London.

Red brick, polished wood, and mullioned windows

beckoned shoppers and diners with stylish nostalgia.

He entered the lobby and veered left to Fuchsia and Lime through heavy wooden doors, looking forward to a seat with a river view. The café walls were all exposed brick, the bar burnished steel and warm polished wood. The bar stools were covered in bright leather, alternating fuchsia and lime, in a long stylish line.

The waitstaff directed him to a corner booth beside a deep stone windowsill. The table was decorated with two cheerful gerberas, one fuchsia and one lime. He traced one long curvy stem with his finger and smiled.

• • •

Kitty hurried through the lobby, on a mission to make five takeaway coffees and get back up to the Sisterhood meeting room ASAP.

She skirted the public queue and dived under the staff swing-doors into the café kitchen. A huge humming, organized space, fragrant with roasting coffee beans and sizzling bacon. It was a workplace she knew well. They all helped out wherever and whenever extra hands were needed.

The kitchen-based coffee machine was all ready for rush-hour use, and Kitty set to work. The coffees were another part of their Sunday ritual. They all ordered the kind of thick, syrupy, creamy drinks that screamed indulgence and special occasion.

She wedged them securely into a takeaway tray, waved good-bye to the kitchen staff, and took her turn in the service queue to leave the kitchen. As she stepped aside for a speedy young waitress expertly carrying four large plates of crispy bacon and creamy eggs, she let her eyes wander over the busy café.

One of the young waitstaff, smart and casual in her logo

T-shirt and black pants, walked away from the far corner booth, her order book in hand.

Her customer was Rosco Redmond.

The Rosco Redmond Kitty imagined was quietly breakfasting with his aunts in Wheatbridge Village.

Her body fizzed hot then cold at the sight of him. She steadied the coffee tray with both hands as all concentration deserted her.

Her instinct was to flee back to her meeting unseen. Not the most mature or businesslike response.

Instead she took a sensible breath, clutched the coffees as her getaway strategy, and walked briskly across the café.

"Rosco," she said, working hard to ignore the tummy-fluttering effect of his liquid-blue eyes. Their make-believe, stud-enhancing day was over, and real life didn't include more kissing and dancing with Rosco. "I haven't had time to work on the wedding album or my Bedouin project. I didn't expect to hear from you until next week."

"I couldn't resist seeing Brick Square for myself." He looked around. "It's impressive. I also wanted to thank you for all your hard work and support at the wedding. You don't look as if you've just gone ten rounds with my aunts and the media."

Kitty laughed, feeling her cheeks warm, as she remembered how much she had enjoyed the process of beating the aunts.

"It was nothing," she said. "Under-the-table business best forgotten." She winked to soften the dismissal.

He looked so in control, so confident in a coal-black leather jacket. So sexy and casual compared to his usual suited elegance, and her fingers itched to caress the expensive butter-soft leather. Yet he was so not for her. All that family solidarity and relationship expectations.

"I have a business proposition for the Sisterhood," he said.

Heavens, she'd told him too much under that table. With Brick Square's public profile growing, she knew better than to speak too personally. "That's an insider term," she said sharply.

He nodded and plowed on, single-focused. "I want to publish a book about Brick Square, its history and development. It would be good publicity. Controlled marketing."

"That's an interesting offer, thank you. I'll mention it to the others." No promises. He gave her a dark look, clearly expecting a more positive response. He was used to having his way in business. She raised her coffee tray. "Everyone's waiting for these. Enjoy your brunch." She smiled a polite good-bye.

He ignored the hint, eyeballing her with the searing intensity she'd witnessed when he'd talked about the way his father treated his mother. "I'll be here for an hour. Come back with your answer."

She absorbed the intensity, merely nodded, and walked away without looking back, aware that he would be watching her. It shouldn't matter, but she wished she'd made more of an effort than jeans and ballet flats.

What should matter more was the dictatorial way he assumed her compliance.

She forced her business sense to brush off her annoyance. Even here on her own ground, he held the commercial power. She was still his employee, she still needed him to look at her Bedouin proposal.

And his latest idea was a marketing gift. Her mind raced as she whizzed up the private elevator to their third floor meeting room and apartments.

The turret room, with its panoramic view of the Thames and the city beyond, was alive with laughter when she opened the door, and her sisters clamored for the coffee as she placed the tray on the table.

Kitty joined them and sipped her latte. She loved this huge corner room with its deep-set windows, rich velvet drapes, and comfortable oversized furniture. The color scheme was ruby rich with her oldest sister, Rosa's, favorite colors—every shade between crimson and peony pink—warm, cozy, and stylish.

The enormous antique dining table doubled as their boardroom, and Rosa stretched across it, flicking each sister a copy of their meeting agenda. She settled in a chair at the head of the table and removed the plastic lid from her spicy chai. "Heavenly," she said, inhaling the vanilla and cinnamon blend. "Let's start with you, Kitty." Rosa grinned knowingly at her. "We're relieved to see you survived your wedding boot camp."

Kitty grinned back at them all as their laughter teased her. They knew only too well how she felt about happily-ever-after statistics.

"Any other business news from you?"

"Rosco Redmond is downstairs eating breakfast. He wants to offer us a publishing contract to record Brick Square's history and restoration."

"Nice one," said Danni, their irrepressible youngest sister. "You must have taken some prizewinning wedding photos." She licked the whipped cream on her mocha while teasing Kitty with a wickedly raised eyebrow.

Kitty knew better than to rise to the bait of that eyebrow. "Rosco wasn't impressed with me at first, probably still thinks I need editorial supervision."

She kept it cool because she didn't want her sisters to sense how being in Rosco's arms had crumbled away a little of her usual boundaries.

Her body had its own ideas about boundaries when Rosco pulled it close.

She shivered and sipped her coffee. Her sisters also didn't

need to know how the photos on the media sites worried her.

It was okay for the image of her as an anonymous guest in Rosco's house to be out there, but there was a risk of her past making a belated splash on social media. Those sites hadn't been around to stalk people with such malicious focus when Kitty was sixteen and her mother had died so controversially. She'd worked too hard for her self-respect to have her adulthood tainted by the salacious details of her mother's life.

"Does this project include you as photographer?" asked Tessa, pulling her back to the present.

"He didn't offer any details."

"Would he actually give us control over the publicity?" asked Meg.

"I'll need to find out. He wouldn't suggest it if he didn't consider it a good business proposition for his publishing house."

"We need an official proposal to tie all the details down," Rosa said, and opened a file on her laptop. "Are we all agreed we should follow this up?" she asked. Everyone nodded their assent.

"Proceed with caution," added Meg.

Kitty barely listened to the rest of the meeting, her mind a kaleidoscope of Rosco images.

Her gut-clenching reaction to the childhood memories his townhouse evoked.

His dismissal of her ability.

His driven protection of his family's well-being, rigid beyond her understanding.

The light in his eyes when he spoke to his little niece.

The way a smile and a kiss on his lips transformed the hard planes of his face.

All the unanswered questions about his leg injury, and Ethel's sadness and concern for him.

The way they all loved each other, caught—Kitty thought

with a shudder—in a complicated web of emotion and obligation.

• • •

Rosco watched Kitty glide across the café toward him and slip into his booth. His gut tightened as she pulled herself along the seat opposite him. It was the same sensation as the moment she'd put her arms around his neck on the dance floor, hauling him closer.

It didn't feel fake. His body's response was real, then and now. The kind of attraction he needed to control—it was the path of risk his father would have taken without a second thought. Mixing business and sexual attraction.

"I don't have any time to spare," Kitty said, the laughter and flirt missing from her eyes. "There are two points I want to cover."

"Shoot," he said, his gut still clenched in response to this Sunday-morning-casual Kitty filling his senses in the confines of the booth, just as she had under that damn table.

"The Brick Square contract is a possibility."

"Good." He nodded. "I'll send you a written proposal. And your second point?"

"The paparazzi," she said, her eyes looking directly at him.

"You've seen our repeat appearance online." He searched her face to gauge her thoughts. "No fresh photos or news."

"No. But I'm stuck with being your mystery woman." She folded her arms across her chest. "What's going on?"

"Nothing to worry about. The Sandford's approve of my media presence with you—whoever you are." He pulled a face, acknowledging her gathering annoyance. "It means they appreciate I have a private life that doesn't include the pop star world."

"How lovely for you."

He ignored her edge of sarcasm. "I need you to continue to be on call as my discreet mystery woman until the palace deal is completed."

"What do you mean?" She glared at him. Not a trace of humor. "I'm not available for public consumption."

He hadn't expected such a vehement response and decided to keep the possibility of a private meeting with the duke to himself.

"Purely theoretical. If the Titania insinuations blow up again I might need another anonymous sighting of us."

"We agreed my decoy days ended with the wedding," she said, unknowingly needling his guilt about protecting her.

The lively passion he was becoming addicted to flared briefly in her eyes but was all too quickly replaced by anger. "You've set me up."

The hair on the back of his neck bristled as she pushed herself out of the booth, then leaned in to maintain privacy. "I'll put up with our photos being rehashed. But I'll have nothing to do with the duke and Trinity St. George. I don't want to be the target of new publicity."

The look in her eye was combative but again held a hint of fear as she pulled away. "Must go. Got a wedding to wrap up. And then..." She pinned him in her sights. "I will be presenting my Bedouin proposal directly to you. You owe me now."

"One step at a time," he said, ignoring an answering stab of guilt.

"I won't dance to your tune like Cara poised on your shoes. If I'm still your decoy, I will say when and where we go and whom I meet."

She sped across the restaurant, anger in her stride. More than ever, he needed to check her out. His morning coffee turned bitter on his tongue as he drained his cup and plotted his next step.

Chapter Ten

Kitty ignored the lift and sprinted up the three flights of stairs to her studio apartment. She needed to burn off her anger and fear. She wouldn't let Rosco's alpha male games or the hideous threat of Trinity St. George taint her editing.

Locking herself away, she unwound as her work focus took over. She spent the rest of Sunday and half the night proofing and refining Amanda and Andrew's wedding album.

The work continued all through Monday as meals were sent up from Fuchsia and Lime, and regular sugar hits were delivered from Meg's bakery. By Monday evening Kitty had digital galleries ready and presentation albums completed. She stretched her tired muscles and ran one last click-through journey of her favorite galleries.

Not bad work for a wedding-phobic. She high-fived her computer screen and emailed everything to Rosco and the bride and groom.

Time to party, she texted her sisters. *First and last ever wedding a done deal.* She added a manic-looking smiley face and tapped send.

Immediately Danni's text replied, *Sorry. No can do. Painting class working overtime for exhibition.*

Rosa's text replied for herself and Meg. *Congrats. Meg and I can't leave client function. Have a red for us.*

Tessa was at the gym, training for her next marathon. *No red wine for her, either*, thought Kitty, pulling an *eeew* face, imagining the raw eggs and green juices Tess called "muscle fuel."

Heels and wine, Kitty decided. She'd hit the shower, dress up for fun, and party on her own.

She pampered herself head to toe, wriggled into a short red dress Danni had found for her on some designer sale rack, stepped into matching red stilettos, and checked her emails one last time.

Rosco Redmond. Did the man never switch off?

Then a little smile lifted her lips and chased a memory of kisses and dancing down her spine. Yes, he was *very* capable of switching off. Briefly. When given the right sort of supervision.

He acknowledged receipt of her album. And now he wanted a meeting to develop the Brick Square proposal.

Not everyone was a workaholic, didn't he know? She sighed and sent back a response. *I'll be in the bar at Brick Square*, she typed and then took the elevator down to the lobby. She doubted he'd be willing to leave his office building on a Monday night, but if the proposal was important enough to him, he could meet her here.

This was her private world. Safe from media intrusion.

Monday night at the bistro bar was busy but not chaotic. She chose a bar stool and waved hello to the bar staff.

She had sipped her way through her first glass of red wine and felt the tensions of the week roll off her when a deep voice with a familiar honeyed lilt came from behind her. "Another glass of Kitty's favorite red, please. And a Coke."

"Rosco?" Kitty swiveled on her bar stool. His strong

face had been on her screen all day. So serious in most of the wedding shots, guarded, nothing like the tenderness she had glimpsed in their under-the-tablecloth world.

He'd brought the guarded look with him tonight, along with a sharp city suit and a briefcase.

"This isn't the usual sort of place for business meetings," he said. "Rather public, isn't it?"

Was he worried about the paparazzi catching them together at a bar that wasn't so posh? She tried to brush off her annoyance. She hadn't asked to meet him tonight. "Were you close by?" She was surprised to see him so soon, or to see him at all really.

"Yes, I wanted to assess the complex at night. Absorb the atmosphere." He rested his briefcase on the bar stool beside her. "You're alone?"

"Yes, just me. I'm celebrating the end of a particularly long project of the happily-ever-after kind." She looked back at the bar, checking if their drinks were ready, needing something to do with her hands.

When she swiveled back, Rosco's disapproving eyes were looking at her dress and it spun her back to their first meeting, when he'd had nothing but criticism for her. When she hadn't felt good enough for him. "So, why have you joined me?"

"I've written my proposal for the Brick Square history project and signed the confidentiality form." He tapped his briefcase. "I was hoping to finalize our agreement."

"That was quick work."

"We have many differences, Kitty, but we're both hard workers." His taut jaw revealed the pain those differences apparently caused him. He had the same expression the first time he'd looked down on her from his front door. "I'd like to think we could work together on this."

She liked the sound of progress, but she wasn't ready to let him off his judgmental hook just yet. It was kind of nice to see his usual controlled self squirm a bit. He was clearly a fish out of water at a bar on the wrong side of town. "Tell me about our differences," she said. "As you see them."

• • •

"Party girl," he said, her scrap of a dress too much for the business detachment he'd promised himself. He had thought about insisting they meet at his office or some other more appropriate venue. But this meeting was his window into her world. To assess how well they could work together. But he couldn't control that Redmond hormonal reaction to her. The attraction he loved and hated in equal measure.

She stiffened, her eyes narrowing, and took her time answering. "I thought you looked disapproving, Rosco. Now you sound it, too." She waited a beat, staring him down. "Do you have some comment to make about my appearance?"

Neon bright, dangerously so, he thought. He cleared his throat to regain control of his words. "You look beautiful."

"And that's a bad thing?"

"No. But the dress and a public bar are not ideal for a business meeting." He looked around as another group of customers crowded around them ordering drinks. "Let's go somewhere private."

"You chose the time," she bit back at him. That was true.

He merely nodded his agreement, raised an eyebrow to reinforce his request for a change of venue, and stood his ground. He didn't want to lose the advantage of surprise, and he did want inside her world, sooner rather than later.

She pursed her lips in reply, obviously annoyed, as she wriggled down from the bar stool. "All right, Mr. Redmond. My apartment," she said. "I want privacy to discuss business, too."

She crooked her finger at him. "Walk this way." Rosco

willingly followed her high-heeled sway—long, strong, and curvy—as she led him out of the bar to the vast internal lobby.

Soft, old-fashioned street lighting made it an inviting place for customers, and her heels clicked across the stone cobbles, a seductive rhythm he couldn't ignore.

Kitty swiped her key card to a private lift and pulled aside the antique metal-gated doors, and he stepped in after her. The space was large, with several bags of flour and a chest of drawers stacked against the walls.

"This is bigger than I expected."

"We kept the original external look but have installed a new mechanism. This is a service lift for Meg's bakery and Danni's gallery on the second floor, and it has locked access to our apartments on the third floor."

He placed his briefcase at his feet, giving Kitty his full attention. Brick Square fascinated him almost as much as Kitty herself.

The lift bumped them to a gentle stop, but Kitty didn't move to open the door. She turned to face him and leaned back, one stilleto braced against the wall behind her. "My dress?" she challenged, taking a slow sip of wine and eyeballing him over the rim. "You were saying…"

Too sexy, he wanted to say but knew it would only fuel whatever fire he had ignited in her. She was gorgeous. He didn't get why she was so touchy about comments on her appearance.

"You look as if you're ready to dance every night. My dancing days are limited to my sisters' weddings."

"Poor Rosco. No more sisters," she said, sugar-sweet. "I get it." She leaned forward. Red bra tonight. He forced himself to look away, back to her eyes.

"You do?" He hoped not.

"Our under-the-table time was the reaction to those extraordinary circumstances. The dancing was a make believe

Ethel-deterrent?" Kitty queried.

"Yes, my thoughts exactly. And the paparazzi following you added another dimension to all that."

"For the last time, they didn't follow me. They were hunting you."

He wasn't giving her a total pass on that one until he knew her secrets. She looked more like tabloid fodder than he did, *and* she was a Brick Square heiress. "But I'm not the one wearing short skirts in the photos, nor am I the offspring of Ralph Kingston."

"The media doesn't know who I am," she snapped. "And I've worked hard to keep it that way." She cradled her wineglass, took a small sip, savored it. Then speared him with her heated brown eyes. "*You* get this," she said just above a whisper. "I might enjoy dressing up and dancing. I might have enjoyed the fun of flirting against what I saw as the injustice of your family's intrusion into your private life." She took a steadying breath and glared at him again. Another slow sip of wine didn't seem to soothe her, and she continued with the same whispered force. "But I am *not* a party girl in any other sense you may, or may not, have implied. If we are going to work together, you need to know that. I don't do 'forever,' but I don't do 'just for tonight,' either. Agreeing to meet here isn't an invitation to my bedroom."

"Understood," he shot right back to reassure her. "I guess that makes me, by definition, not a 'party boy,' either."

He gulped an ice-cold mouthful of his Coke. He wasn't used to being questioned by a woman. He was used to being the one doing the vetting and boundary setting.

Kitty kept surprising him. In a good way.

"You've inherited your father's legendary straight shooting, for sure," he told her. "Tell it like it is when the chips are down skills."

"I wouldn't say that," she almost snarled, still angry, still distrusting.

He'd been doing a little Kingston family research. No reason why Kitty should have a more comprehensive picture of his family than he had of hers.

It was reassuringly free of gossip. He'd found nothing about her mother, but her father had been an early mover and shaker in the London docklands restoration. Articles cited him as a tough negotiator with a determined focus on detail. His five daughters attested to a complicated personal life, but he appeared to have kept it private.

He took another swallow, tamping down his temper. "I only meant the comparison as a business compliment."

His conscience niggled as he looked at her skeptical face. It was uncomfortably true that he was checking her out. "I'm not questioning your morals, just your dress sense for our mystery woman charade."

He risked stepping even closer to her, into the heat gathering between them. He wanted that heat to be positive. "I love your dress sense." What man wouldn't? "But it is attention-grabbing for any lurking paparazzi. My only agenda for this evening is to discuss business."

He watched her eyes burn brown-black as she considered him, and he saw the moment she decided he was telling the truth and to let him into her home.

She opened the lift door and raised her wineglass in a toast, giving him one of the twinkly, fun-loving grins that turbocharged his hormones. "Follow me," she said with that kick of flirt his body loved. "My apartment is usually a no-go area."

"Untidy?" Slam dunk. He could afford to tease.

She laughed. "Careful. I can always un-invite you."

She led him to a recessed wooden door. Solid, with a carved surround and ornate iron latch.

"We're on the third floor above the businesses," she said,

unlocking the door. "We each have an apartment with a view of the city and the Thames."

She opened her door into a short hallway, polished wooden floors, exposed brick structural walls, and one of the huge exterior arched windows at the end. He could just make out a few twinkling city lights in the distance.

Her heels clicked along the wooden floor, switching on subdued lighting as she turned out of the hallway.

"Welcome to my world, Rosco," she said.

"I love it." It looked as stylish as her—open plan, the brick riverside wall with its line of arched windows all open to the view.

The large space was divided by furniture and shelving cubes into dining, living, and office spaces. Wooden floors, soft gray walls, white furniture, and rusty-orange cushions.

He roamed, as her obvious pride allowed him the opportunity to be nosy, to get up close to her work.

Some of her Jabbering Gerbera artwork and historical photographs were hung in white recessed shelving. It had the sparse appearance of an art gallery, softened by the full-length wall of exposed brick.

He loved it. The unique quality and presentation of her work was exciting to his publisher's eye. Work which was worthy of inclusion in his late mother's company.

"To business," he said, not wasting a moment of the small truce between them. He walked farther into the apartment, to the office area, where everything was ordered and tidy.

Kitty had several large desks arranged together, and one was obviously for her Jabbering Gerbera work, as a vampish orange eye screen saver winked at him.

He smiled despite himself, unable to resist its seductive cartoon charm as he placed his briefcase on a work table and selected a file. "Brick Square contract and your signed confidentiality agreement." He handed her two signed copies, willing her to cooperate.

Attraction, respect, a hint of guilt, all engulfed him, and he didn't want to lose this contract, or her, from his life.

"Good." She took the papers. "We'll be tough negotiators," she warned with a small smile, teasing him now, and something shifted inside him. The possibility of life without the reserve he'd built around his heart beckoned in the light of her smile and the wink of her Gerbera Girl eye.

• • •

Kitty took the papers, aiming for businesslike detachment but worried her heart was leading her head as she assessed his direct blue gaze. She wanted this contract for all of them, but she was wary of the passions Rosco was stirring in her.

"It's solid, Kitty. My word. My integrity."

And she knew that was true. Instinctively knew. Another factor threatening her resistance to him.

"Yes," she said, her voice more husky than intended. He stood, tall and lean, beside her. His sexiness refined, once again, by expert tailoring.

"Sit down," she said, gesturing to the nearest office chair as she sat next to him. He seemed less overwhelming sitting down. "Tell me about your proposal."

"There are three layers. First, the architectural and social history of the building complex."

She nodded. "We have quite a bit of photographic work done on that already."

"The short montage on your website is a good start. Is that some of your work?"

"Yes." Warmed by his compliment, she relaxed further. "I've taken all the photographs since I arrived eighteen months ago."

"So you have documented all development?"

"Yes, and Rosa has quite a bit of historical material. Black and white photos and some amazing letters and journals."

"I can engage researchers to follow that up."

"No. Rosa will want to be in charge of that aspect. She used to come here as a child, and she lived here for a short time as a teenager. The history is incredibly personal for her."

"Good. That's exactly the sort of thing I need to know. I want to project manage to achieve the very best result."

Kitty tapped the table between them, polished and smooth beneath her fingers. She was close enough to absorb his intensity as he wrote notes in the margins of his proposal.

His jaw was shadowed with end-of-day stubble, his face businesslike and handsome. She looked away; he embodied distraction.

Although she laughed along with Danni's jokey "hunk-o-meter" evaluations of guys, celebrities and friends alike, Kitty was seldom swayed by manly magnetism.

On the rare occasion she had allowed it to happen, she'd then felt pressured for more commitment than she could give, was born to give, and she'd moved on. Literally.

There had always been a new country to explore. New people to meet.

"Next layer?"

"Your businesses. Wonderful mix of services. Wonderful names." He smiled at her. "Jabbering Gerbera isn't easily forgotten."

"Charmer."

"Just calling it as I see it." He traced a cross over his heart, the sleeve of his jacket brushing the bare skin of her arm.

He sat so close, so tempting. Handsome, intelligent, and boyish when he forgot to be serious.

"That's a big topic—involves all five of us. And we're all different."

"A can of worms?" More serious now, less boyish.

Agreeing would feel disloyal. "I can only speak for myself. Not a problem, but definitely a group decision."

"Okay. Does that translate to a no?"

"No." She laughed, leaving everything personal unsaid. "But it is a very drawn-out yes. We're constantly discussing and planning our advertising and publicity, but we haven't considered working with outside agencies."

She looked at him, and his eyes, a sincere blue, looked back. Sincere blue eyes. The wine thinking, she decided. Just as long as it didn't start talking.

"Some of us tolerate personal publicity more than others. That's all I'm saying."

"Ah..." He considered her, completely serious now, and sucked on his lower lip. "That impacts on layer three."

Kitty mirrored his action, chewing her own lip, unable to forget how kissing his mouth had felt. How inconveniently kissable she found it now.

"Which is?"

"Your personal histories, the worldwide search. The whole Kingston dynasty story."

She chilled to the bone. "No." Hell would freeze over before she and Meg would tolerate that.

"Readers love the inside story of the real people, the personalities behind the empire."

"You're being hypocritical," she snapped, leaning even closer.

He held his hands up at her reaction. "Think about it."

"Hypocrite," she repeated, her face so close to his she could see the diamond chips in his blue-blue eyes. "Mr. Bald and Anonymous on your own website."

"We're talking about your family's publication, not mine." His voice held its steely edge, and Kitty had a glimpse of how formidable he must be in his boardroom meetings. Did he always get the terms he wanted?

"Wouldn't you be worried about how my family story, skeletons and all, might impact your business dealings now that we're linked together?"

"Your identity is still a mystery to the paps, and our fake romance will be over by then. My deal will be signed and sealed very soon." He seemed to remind himself of their arrangement then as he whispered, "Under table confidentiality oath still active." He leaned forward, his eyes on hers. "We both experienced death and trauma way too early. This deal won't hurt you or your sisters."

She sat completely still, her eyes locked with his. His mention of their time under the tablecloth had her imagining him kissing her again. The air around them buzzed with shared emotion, and she shuddered as she pulled away. She wanted him. But the balm of a kiss around their shared anger wouldn't answer her questions. Wouldn't keep her safe.

"Tell me about your hair," she murmured after a moment to catch her breath, needing to stop this tide of very nonworkplace emotion.

"I look like my father," he said "Same hair."

"You shaved him off."

She pulled away, giving Rosco's rich brown hair her full attention.

"Did it help?" She was certainly glad she had never looked anything like her mother.

"It didn't make me any happier," he said after a few moments of thought. His voice caressed her name with that subtle Irish lilt that kept curling her toes. "I was still me." He smiled softly at her. "And my memories of my father stayed the same." He shrugged his shoulders. "You can't change the past at the barber's." Again, a soft smile. "But it was a relief, at the time, to put a photo on the website that looked nothing like him. I needed to project some difference between myself and his alcoholic legacy."

"I can understand that." More than he knew.

"Not enough to shave your head, I hope," he said, turning toward her and looping a tendril of her long dark hair through his fingers, tugging gently.

"My feelings about *my* father aren't that strong." She laughed; at least that was true. She didn't have a relationship with Ralph, so no memories there to haunt her, and her initial anger had faded as Brick Square life had warmly enveloped her.

Her sisters had changed her life; she didn't need to run away anymore. Brick Square would always be home. A safe place to negotiate risk.

Rosco gently pulled her hair again, returning her attention to him as his tug pulsed deep inside her. "Vanity wins at the hairdressers for me," she whispered, linking her fingers with his, still tangled in the fall of her hair.

She lifted her other hand, ran her fingers through his silky waves, pushed them off his forehead, then smoothed the waves back into their usual style. "Don't shave it again."

The air between them thickened with desire, and she let it build. Delicious and distracting from business. She moved farther away from him, sat back in her chair. Keeping her hands off him was easier when there was some distance between them. "You'll need to convince me of this project before I even worry the others. It's my contract to approve."

She watched his pupils dilate. "I'm offering you a huge opportunity to boost your businesses," he said.

"Yes, you are. But you're also planning to use our story to make a profit."

He regarded her with gratifying respect. "It's business, yes. But exploitation? No."

"I intend to ensure it isn't. I'll be writing my own version of this proposal and watching out for any exploitation clauses in yours."

"No contest, Kitty." He grinned, confident and in charge. "I'll argue every point with total integrity."

"Brave man," she said, his teasing eyes giving a whole new meaning to blue-sky thinking. "Lots of fighting ahead of us."

"Yes. And respect," he said, pulling her up from her seat. "And fun."

"You approve of fun? I'm shocked." She placed her hand over her chest where the low cut of her little red dress had disturbed him.

"I'm not as prudish as our paparazzi decoy rules suggest." His hand moved up to caress her cheek. "That's all for the cameras. But the private kissing was real." His thumb outlined her mouth. Stoking her desire. "Yes?"

Attraction trumped caution when she was safe in her own home with this complexly principled man who was too hot to ignore. Her heart skipped a beat as his eyes held hers, and the world shrank to the caress of his skin on hers.

His thumb continued to circle. "You're in charge."

She kissed the palm of his hand, his skin warm against her lips. "You undermine all my best business instincts. Do you know that?"

He moved his fingers to run them through the silky fall of her hair. "I know exactly what you mean." Then he stood and took her hand, pulling her up. "We need to be somewhere more comfortable."

He'd said she was in charge, but she felt anything but sure of herself. Her body wanted him in her bed, but her head and heart counseled caution.

She kept hold of his hand, strong and assured in hers. "Walk this way," she said, leading him away from the bedroom toward the sofa.

"Can't. Haven't got the heel height for it," he deadpanned.

She turned, loving the humor he used to settle her nerves, and he pulled her against his chest. His kiss was hot, urgent, and he took charge as his mouth possessed hers.

Her response was instant, blistering through her reserve and anxieties as her mouth melted against his.

With one arm he held the length of her body tight to his, with the other hand he cupped the back of her head. She had no room to move, yet, desperate to be even closer, she molded herself to him.

He cocooned her body, bending her backward in the dance of desire they hadn't indulged in at the wedding. He groaned, wrenching his mouth from hers and moved down to her neck.

She wriggled, mewed in complaint, as her mouth missed the attentions of his, and threaded her hands up into the thick waves of his hair. She thought she wanted more kissing, but as he lowered his lips to nuzzle her breasts, her body told her she was wrong.

The rasp of his jaw blazed across her flesh, and she wanted him everywhere. He seemed to understand, to feel the same as he loosened his grasp and his hands began to roam her body.

This was nothing like the gentle care she'd felt under the tablecloth. This was a tidal wave of shared sensation, of need. His hands followed the curves of her body, up over her hips, resting at her waist as his mouth nestled between her breasts. He murmured her name, and then, blessedly, returned his mouth to hers.

She clung wildly, never wanting him to move away again, as his hands claimed her breasts, and the kissing dissolved reality.

She lost track of time and place until he slowed the kiss and pulled his mouth from hers. They were both breathing heavily, their bodies still entwined as he pressed his lips gently along her hairline.

"I want you without the dress, Kitty." He stroked her hair,

cradled her head to his chest. Gentle again.

Yes, her body shouted at her. *Yes. Now.*

"No," she whispered, nuzzling her head against his neck. "Not yet," she added, to lessen the rejection.

He was overwhelming. Maybe he could mix business and pleasure, as long as it was private. But she knew she couldn't.

He nodded, and they stayed in each other's arms, cooling down like two well-raced horses, reluctant to leave the thrill of their chase.

He continued to cradle her head, occasionally caressing the length of her hair as she linked her hands at his neck, holding on to the last threads of their passion.

Finally, she shivered, reluctant to leave his arms but needing time away from him. Time to assert her usual independent self and get back to normal life.

She wanted to work with Rosco, but there was no way she should allow this delicious temptation to continue.

Slowly they drew apart, and Rosco collected his briefcase.

"You've been the perfect guest," she teased, leading him to the door.

"I aim to please."

He walked with his hand at her back, and she reveled in these last few minutes of contact because she knew it was something she couldn't let happen again.

"I'll call you in a week," she said, unlocking the lift for him. "I have a couple of new projects to work on for a very picky publisher."

"A week is a long time. Too long."

She smiled at him as the doors closed. "We're busy; it will go quickly enough."

"I very much doubt that. I'll be in touch."

Chapter Eleven

Rosco gave Kitty two days before dialing her work cell phone.

"I'm picking you up for lunch," he said when she answered. "You need a break." *And I need to see you,* he thought, stirring his favorite one-pot lamb recipe.

He'd received insinuating emails about his business ethics, and the tabloid photos of Kitty were attached.

He was sure they were from his Sandford Palace contract opponent—rubbish aimed solely at him to undermine his business nerve. He didn't plan to tell Kitty unless he had to, knowing how she felt about her privacy.

And he needed to ensure she would agree to accompany him to a Sandford Palace interview if the duke and his wife insisted on meeting him and his "mystery woman" before they finalized their selection for a publisher. He wouldn't rush into appealing for her help with that, but if necessary he would convince her. Her creative talent and natural poise would be a natural fit for any Sandford Palace meetings.

Leaning against the countertop in his townhouse kitchen, he imagined her sitting at her giant computer screen, refining her digital work. "Are you Gerbera Girl at the moment, or Kitty Mayfair?" he asked.

• • •

Kitty's heart leapt at the sound of his voice. She'd been thinking of him and didn't want him to hear any attraction in her response.

"Who's speaking?" she asked, buying some simmer-down time. "I can't just take off for lunch with any unknown man."

"It's the person who knows you eat muesli bars and drink red wine under tables."

"Hmm… Is that a threat?" she asked in a stage whisper. "That's the sort of information that could ruin my professional credibility. I have a contract with Rosco Redmond to protect."

"Ah. Rosco. A complicated man." He clicked his tongue. "Your only hope to save your reputation is to meet me for lunch."

The laughter in his voice licked at her desire. She should resist, but temptation won. "How will I recognize you?"

"I'll be on the river path in thirty, carrying gerberas."

"What color gerberas?"

"Orange and yellow."

"Nice." Her favorite flowers and lunch. Who *could* resist?

"Don't keep me waiting," he said.

"Will we be walking far?" She was already planning what to wear. Heels, definitely, if they weren't trekking.

"Just to the car."

"Okay." She ended the call, hit save on her computer, and scrambled, laughing, toward her wardrobe. She wasn't letting his sexy blue gaze tempt her beyond a working relationship. But he was always so put together, her home office sweats wouldn't do.

She riffled through the rack, and the oversized orange

zipper of the lacy shift she'd worn at the wedding snagged her attention with good memories. Her inner vamp *had* been over-egged that evening with Ethel-inspired injustice. She laughed out loud as she stripped off her sweats.

Now. Favorite black leggings, favorite black boots, new black bra, and the same lacy shift. Perfect.

She smoothed the fitting lines of the outfit and opted for color over the black. The long chili red-swing coat she shared with Rosa.

The coat's high neck buttoned up over the orange zipper and its maxi length covered her boots. Kitty stuck her hands in the coat's deep pockets to twirl in front of the mirror for maximum swing. City living with four new sisters had certainly upgraded her wardrobe and encouraged her new infatuation with high heels.

Satisfied, she threw her wallet and phones and keys into a bright red tote, took the private lift to the ground floor, and slipped among the lunchtime shoppers heading for the river path.

The wind blew the first autumn leaves at her feet, and she concentrated on the uneven flagstones taking her down to the river.

There, leaning on the iron railings, with the dark river behind him, stood a man in a long black coat, with his collar turned up against the wind, watching her.

He carried the biggest bunch of gerberas Kitty had ever seen, all yellow and orange, and arranged in a goldfish bowl.

Rosco.

Kitty's breath caught at the sight of him. His grin softened those chiseled features, drawing her to him. She threw caution to the autumn breeze and ran the last few steps between them.

He wrapped one arm tightly around the glass bowl and reached out to offer her a one-armed hug. She stepped into the embrace, and they kissed both of each other's cheeks. It would look like they were just old friends to any watching eyes, but her lips quivered with the need to devour him, and she felt that same intensity in the way his eyes met hers.

How quickly that rapport had grown. She felt light as air, and his sparkling blue eyes told her he felt the same.

It felt so good she was tempted to ignore all her misgivings about the risks a personal relationship with Rosco represented. The paparazzi focus, the family complexities, the need to explain her distasteful family history.

This was just a companionable business lunch. She'd enjoy it.

"The flowers are beautiful," she said, stepping away to avoid crushing them. "Wherever did you find so many?"

"Three florists and a pet shop." He tapped the glass bowl with successful shopper's pride.

"Great shopping skills for a boy," she teased, hiding a niggle of unease. A huge bouquet of colorful flowers would attract attention from anyone. He must be very confident their threat of paparazzi was over. Or, even more worrying, he was hoping for more photos to be leaked now that a "mystery woman" was good for his image. She tried to brush off that thought—surely not. He hated the paps, too.

She stroked the soft petals of one sunshine-yellow flower. It looked far too innocent to be anything other than a genuine gift acknowledging their private time together.

"Learned the shopping secrets from my sisters," he explained. "I was a useful bag carrier on their expeditions."

He pointed across the walkway toward the street. "The car is just around the corner."

The wind ruffled his brown hair, and he looked boyish and carefree as he led her to the car, waited while she belted in, and handed her the flowers to balance on her knee.

"Are you all right," she asked. "I've been worried about your Sandford Palace bid." She needed to know the latest.

That paparazzi episode was still unsettling.

"Still waiting on the palace contract. But I'm being proactive about new contracts, as you know." He smiled at her, teasing again.

"I won't let you forget my Bedouin project," she said, watching his face carefully, so close to hers in the car. Was it risky for them to be out in public together? She hadn't thought to check for paps when they'd met on the bridge. "You'll tell me if there are any more gossip snaps I should be warned about?"

She felt him pause and searched his profile for the truth. "I don't have any new details." He turned to face her with concern and a touch of temper firming his mouth. "I wish I could guarantee the future, but I can't. So far, there haven't been any new photos of us, and I haven't seen a camera anywhere."

"Thank goodness. I haven't found anything more online, either." Kitty allowed herself to be partially reassured as he pulled the car out into the traffic, but their vulnerability to future gossip nagged at her. And Trinity St. George would always be a potential threat.

She took a deep, deliberately relaxing breath as the leather interior of Rosco's low silver coupe enveloped her in quiet comfort.

"Cool car," she said, blocking out the rest of the world. "Nothing like the noisy, you-know-you're-driving-an-old-classic juddering of my little Dolly."

"Your Citroën looks just right for you." He grinned but kept his concentration on the traffic. "How long have you had it?"

"Long time. Long story," she said, wishing she hadn't introduced the subject. She knew Rosco wouldn't let it drop, so she continued. "It was my first big buy before I took off around the world. I left it with a friend for years." He didn't need to know how much she loved it and how much courage it had taken to buy it. To break a two-year stubborn refusal to spend any of the small inheritance left after her mother's house was sold and the debts paid. "I was eighteen and totally into retro."

"Cute and quirky," he said. "Has it got a name?"

Kitty laughed. "Of course."

"Not just Dolly, then?"

"No." She winced. "If I tell you, you have to promise not to laugh."

He crossed his heart when they drew to a stop at traffic lights and turned his mock-serious eyes to hers.

"Buttercup," she said.

"Very appropriate," he said with a nod, tongue-in-cheek.

"I was young. First car love."

"It's such a girl name." He emphasized the "girl" with an adolescent sneer.

"Thanks," she said. "I am a girl. And proud."

"So you should be," he said softly, all mockery gone.

Kitty gave his driver's profile an uneven little smile and turned to look out the window to hide her sudden emotion.

A handsome man to tease her rotten, to make her feel special. Someone to stick up for her when she'd needed it most. She'd never had that in her life. Never missed it. Until now.

The lunchtime traffic passed in a blur, until Rosco turned the car onto a quiet street she recognized immediately. He parked outside his townhouse and turned to her.

"Are you okay," he asked with real concern.

She nodded, realizing how her nerves must show on her face, as all the memories this house brought on reminded her of scenes she'd rather forget. Scenes from childhood and from the paparazzi ambush still fresh and confronting. She thought she'd never have to visit here again.

"Sit there. I'll get the flowers."

• • •

He rounded the front of the car, not taking his eyes off Kitty's tense face.

She looked stunning today, her brown-black hair a glossy fall against the smart red coat. Her eyes had shone with the life and laughter he was beginning to trust. Wanted to trust that they could be friends, that she would, if required, be his willing partner in this relationship ruse to land the Sandford contract.

But suddenly that sparkle had gone. And it didn't take a genius to work out it had something to do with his house and her memories.

All of that was a piece of the Kitty puzzle he intended to solve today.

He opened the car door.

"Why are we here?" she said with a trace of rattling in her voice. "There are tons of restaurants where we can have lunch."

"I don't think either of us wants the paps catching us with spinach in our teeth," he quipped. He held the door open and waited.

She narrowed a glance at him, grudgingly ackowledging he was right, and sprang out of the car. She stalked up the porch steps to wait for him by his front door, glaring at the entrance to his house.

He unlocked it one-handed, grimly hanging on to the glass bowl. The minimal water he'd added to cover the stem tips would be a mini tidal wave if Kitty chose to throw it at him. He tried to keep his tone casual, to calm her down as he placed the flowers on the hall table. "Tell me what's wrong."

Kitty pinched her lips together in silence. He'd give her a

little longer, but he *would* find out her secrets.

"It's just lunch," he said over his shoulder as he strode down the hall.

"Don't walk away from me, Rosco Redmond."

"Too late."

Kitty followed him, her heels click-clacking across the parquet at a racing clip. How did she do that?

"Lamb and rosemary," he said, heading to the kitchen. "You'll like it."

Her heels kept pace. "I'm not hungry."

"I am." He put the kitchen central breakfast bar between them. "Have a seat." He gestured toward the line of high stools, then removed his overcoat and threw it over one of them.

She rammed her hands deep into her coat pockets, glowering at him.

He turned his back, switched on the heat under the pot of pre-cut potatoes, reached above the bench to take a plate from the crockery cupboard.

He didn't want her angry enough to bolt, but he wanted to keep her simmering enough to talk. He might be able to allay her concerns about the latest paparazzi developments if he knew exactly what worried her. Did she really have that much to hide?

She folded her arms, one booted foot tapping, her lips thinning as she considered her response.

The silence festered between them as he put the casserole in the microwave and assembled butter, cream, salt, and pepper for the potatoes. If he was going to be eating them under siege, they were going to be the most decadent he could make them.

Kitty continued to simmer along with the potatoes.

He rifled through the utensil drawer for the masher, then placed it gently beside his ingredients.

"Mister Domesticity," she said, still spoiling for a fight. He ignored the words, decided to ignite the heat.

"I'm the hypocrite who shaved his head, remember, Ms. Tell It Like It Is." He fought to keep his tone mild. How he ached to confront whoever had caused this hurt and anger in her. "It's your turn to talk."

She drew a ragged breath, then the mutinous silence continued.

"Let me tell it like I see it, then." He knifed the potatoes. Cooked. He drained them, added the yummy stuff, and picked up the masher. "You," he said, pointing the masher at her, not flinching from her dark-eyed glare, "are scared of memories you keep locked away in a box that looks a lot like my house."

He mashed forcefully. Metal on metal.

"Mr. Smarty," she said, softer, still hurting.

He piled the mash onto his plate. Shoved on oven gloves, removed his casserole dish from the microwave, and opened the lid.

"Perfect," he inhaled appreciatively.

He ladled a generous portion of lamb onto the plate, poured thick, rich gravy over the mash.

The laden plate would feed them both. He took knife, fork, and plate across the kitchen to a small glass table, pulled out two chairs, and sat at one.

"My mother loved to eat here, looking out to the garden." He didn't turn to look at her, just talked as he loaded his fork. He chewed and swallowed, barely tasting his usual favorite, hoping Kitty would join him.

"It's her family house; she inherited it, so I can be here knowing my father never was."

Slowly, Kitty's heels clicked across the tiles. She slid onto the chair beside him, skewed sideways in the seat, ready to run.

Rosco loaded another forkful. Chewed, enjoyed a hint of

rosemary this time.

Kitty settled back a little in her chair, watchful, but still with him. The next mouthful delivered the full flavor of the lamb as it hit his taste buds.

"When I left here after the pre-wedding shoot, I promised myself I'd never come back," she said, her voice flat.

"Sorry," he said. "Sorry my house upsets you. Sorry I gave you a hard time that day."

He toyed with another juicy piece of lamb. "But I'm not sorry you're here now. Would you have come if I'd told you where we were going for lunch?"

"I don't know."

"I think you would. I would have played the hypocrite with the shaved head card sooner." He risked a grin, snaffled another mouthful.

She smiled ruefully back. "I deserved that."

"You also deserve to eat. Courage, something I suspect you have truckloads of, needs to be fed."

He speared a piece of lamb, held his hand under the gravy-laden morsel, and raised it to her lips.

There was a bit of her sparkly spirit back as she obediently opened her mouth.

"A packet mix, Rosco?"

"Made from scratch," he said mock-outraged, thrilled she was sparring with him again.

"Delicious. More," she commanded, opening her mouth again.

He plied her with gravy-soaked mash and decided to extract some answers to the questions that most worried him.

He held another forkful up to her still stubborn-looking mouth. "What happened on the nights you weren't fed and wanted?" A muscle in his jaw tensed, shooting pain up to his temple. "Were you hurt…?" He left the word "abused" unsaid. Too powerful to say—although he'd deal with it if he had to.

She turned away from the food. "I was sent to the movies. In a taxi."

"You weren't ever hurt?" He had to know what he was dealing with. What she was dealing with.

"No." She shook her head then swept her hair up into a messy coil, repeatedly dragging stray strands up and up, off her taut face.

She gave it one final vicious twist and let it fall. "No need to feel you have to be my big brother, Rosco. I looked after myself."

He tossed the fork onto the plate, the latest mouthful uneaten. "Brotherly is one thing I never feel for you." His temple continued to throb. He rubbed at it in frustration, tossing up where to take this next. To bed? Not yet.

"I refused to show fear, ever," she continued, pride at the edges of hurt. "They did me a favor. I fell in love with film."

"That's when the photography started?" he asked gently. So many gaps, she seemed to have started at the end, but he'd gladly circle with her.

Kitty nodded with the hint of a smile.

"I'm a bit confused." He was convinced the film and photography thing was a red herring. "Why would you show fear at the movies?"

"They sent me in the dark."

"Alone? In a taxi?"

"Yes, but the movie theater people looked after me. They knew who my mother was." She drew a bracing breath. "It was a little art-house theater a few blocks from home. They gave me popcorn."

"How old were you?"

"Ten. Then I went to a country boarding school, joined the photography club, and kept out of my mother's social life."

"Hell, Kitty." Disgust forced him to his feet. "Your mother

and my father were made for each other."

He looked down at her, and his heart clenched. That lovely, lively face looked tired, but there was more to this story.

"I have a challenge for you," he said. Kitty narrowed her eyes at him, but he had her attention. "Walk around this house with me, free up those memories."

"Why?" She morphed into a petulant teenager, twirled a tendril of her hair. Guilt tweaked his conscience as concern for her was equaled by his own caution. He wanted answers for himself.

"Your reward will be to choose a new photo of me for my website."

She stood. "Completely my choice. Or no go."

Heaven help him, he knew he'd have a high price to pay for his "non-brotherly" concern.

"Deal." He took her hand. She didn't resist, so he took the lead. "Let's start where we are. Is this anything like the kitchen you grew up in?"

Chapter Twelve

Kitty transported herself back in time, Rosco's warm hand giving her strength.

She scanned the cream-and-glass room with its adjoining eating area looking over the garden and shook her head. "Our kitchen was small, lots of dark wood, and only one window looking out."

"No bad memories here?"

"No, only bad cooking," she joked to lighten the worry on his face.

He squeezed her hand and led her out toward the foyer. Kitty stiffened. "Not so good for you here?" he said.

"No." She cleared her throat, damned if she was losing this challenge. "No."

"What happened in your foyer?"

Kitty shivered, her overcoat no protection against bitter childhood memories. "It is exactly the same proportions. Same acoustics." She gave Rosco a self-conscious shrug. "We did a lot of yelling at each other when no one else was around. And I wasn't allowed upstairs when guests were there—adults only."

He nodded. No hint of judgment, but the pinch of controlled anger tightened his jaw. "Okay, where did you sleep?"

"Downstairs bedroom." She swung their joined hands, pointing beyond the stairway, and he took her there. She followed, apprehensive. The room had been her haven, but she hadn't always felt safe even there.

Rosco opened the door and a light-filled space made her gasp. "It's beautiful. Same styling as your mother's country house." She walked in slowly.

"We made-over the whole back of the house. Living room and kitchen both made bigger and lighter, and this room was built out into a garden suite for my mother."

"It's lovely. Pretty but unfussy."

"What about yours?"

"Small, dark, covered in posters. My mother said she should have had shares in a doubled-sided sticky tape company."

"She didn't stop you decorating?"

"No. She didn't care as long as I kept out of the way when she had parties, or when her boyfriend of the moment was around." Kitty couldn't hide her sadness.

Rosco squeezed her hand, and Kitty let him keep holding it. It felt safe.

"I didn't have a lock on my door and once, when they forgot to send me away, my mother's drunken boyfriend started yelling at me. I had to drag furniture in front of the door." She closed her eyes and allowed herself to remember.

"Yelling, banging on the door that didn't stop. I had an old set of drawers I pulled the drawers out of, dragged it in front of the door, replaced the drawers, and filled them with all my heaviest books. Just as well I was a reader."

Rosco inhaled sharply as he tightened his fingers around hers again.

"Brave."

Her heart thumped. "I was scared," she whispered. "I was fifteen when it happened and home for the holidays."

"What did you do?"

"I jumped out the window. I'd made a gap in the fence behind the garden shed, so I knew I could escape. No one saw me."

"Then what?"

"I caught the train to boarding school. Joined the holiday group."

Kitty pulled away from Rosco, feeling some of the weight of the past leave her.

"I was lucky. My mother agreed I could stay at the school hostel after that."

Rosco sighed, and she removed her hand from his.

"Back to the foyer," she said, turning on her heel. She didn't want his sympathy before she'd finished re-assembling her past, separating it from his house. "The last time I saw my mother we were screaming at each other from the top and bottom of the stairs."

"Your last memory of your home?"

"Yes. Nearly fifteen years ago." Kitty stopped at the bottom of the stairs. "I never went back." Not after her school counselor and a policeman had accompanied her to collect her belongings. Her mother hadn't stopped them, but she hadn't been happy. Or sober.

"I walked away," she said, climbing up a couple of steps then turning to look down at him. "And I didn't stop until you answered your door, looking sexy and cross and dismissing me with your angry Irish accent."

Rosco looked uncomfortable and about to deny his anger. Kitty raised her hand, palm toward him. "I'm not finished." She frowned at his strong face softened by those brown waves curling softly now, near his collar. "You're a separate challenge, Rosco Redmond. But you're not part of my past."

In fact, she'd never known anyone quite like him. He might not be part of her past, but he was a big part of why she wanted to leave that past behind her now.

Really leave it behind.

Not just run from it. She'd fooled herself about that; she had been running ever since.

She stepped down, back to the marble floor, and walked toward the front door.

"Are you leaving before you've finished?" Rosco asked, challenge roughening his tone.

"No." She turned toward him, irritated he'd think she would. "I'm starting again."

She walked to the hall table and looked at herself in the mirror above it. "My mother was blond and beautiful, the 'It' girl of the catwalk and fashion mags. I've always been glad I don't look like her."

She caught Rosco's eye in the mirror and grinned. "No need to shave my head."

He smiled back, a complication shared.

Kitty undid her coat, posed in front of the mirror, hands on hips. "She taught me how to stand, how to use light, how to make clothes look good." Kitty swung her coat, evaluated her reflection. "Life Skills 101 according to Jacqueline Mayfair. Exhausting stuff, having to look perfect."

The mirror blurred, anger biting again. "I was a cute accessory when I was little. Then I was living proof she was getting older."

She turned back to Rosco. "My mother did her best. She bought her house herself when she was young and famous. She gave me everything money could buy, until she started running out of it. She never meant to hurt me. She never meant for the crazy guys at her parties to hurt me, either, she was just too drunk and stoned to notice."

"You deserved better." Rosco's voice was strong,

affirming, his arms folded across his chest, still standing at the bottom of the stairs. "You were a child."

"I grew up quickly," she said, inspecting her reflection again. "Classic psychological stuff." She sighed, leaning into the mirror. "I have her eyebrows, that's all."

"I'll hide my razor." Dry. She loved his dryness.

"My mother isn't in the mirror. Never has been." Sadness washed through her, a wave of spent emotion. "And she isn't in your house. This space just triggered memories."

"You were a child," he said again, patiently. "You were powerless then. Now you're in charge." He took a step toward her. "Do you want to leave?"

"No. I want to see everything."

She held out her hand to him. She still needed his support. "I'm all talked out. But I'm ready to move on. Show me upstairs." Forbidden adult territory.

• • •

Rosco linked his fingers with hers and walked her up the grand staircase. It was one of the most striking features of these Georgian townhouses; no wonder it had left an impression.

The height and curve of it held its own drama. For a vulnerable, unhappy child the echoes of raised voices and loneliness would have magnified the conflict.

He soothed her hand with his thumb, the rhythm circling with his need for her. A need he could no longer deny. Her ability to grow so strongly from her childhood neglect only increased his admiration for her.

He watched her taking each step beside him, her coat no longer hiding her long legs beneath the same short black dress she'd worn at the wedding.

The orange zipper, closed snug at her neck, tempted him.

He wanted her.

All of her. But not just for a night; definitely not for only lunchtime. Not without really knowing each other first. They weren't there yet.

"Three bedrooms to the left," he said at the top of the stairs. "One bedroom and my office to the right."

• • •

Kitty tried to ignore the sensation of Rosco's thumb caressing her hand. Her response wasn't limited to that one spot. Her whole body began to fizz with little rockets of warmth and desire. She was having another Rosco moment.

She felt a rush of romantic adventure, all new, unchartered, with no guidebook, and free of the past.

Almost.

"Show me your office," she said, feeling suddenly hot in her outdoor coat. She wasn't going anywhere near a bedroom. "You've seen my home studio. I want to see where you work."

It was at the front of the house, a room of gracious proportions, with two rectangular arch-topped windows looking over the cobblestone street below.

"It's beautiful," she said, peeking past the door as Rosco's hand led her slowly into the room. She resisted following him for a moment and their arms stretched apart.

"Your mother designed this for you." There was no doubt in her mind. Designed with love. An entire wall of shelves and cupboards, creamy white, classically solid, faced her.

A massive glass desk with chunky steel supports occupied the back wall and, tucked in behind the door, another floor to ceiling work unit housed all the latest office equipment.

Rosco reeled her in, secured her body next to his. "It's handsome," she said, squeezing his hand.

"Even better with you in it."

"Corny line."

"True, to be sure."

"Ah, you know I love it when you vamp up the Irish." She felt her cheeks flush as her heart leaped to its own River Dance beat and she couldn't stop a grin at her fanciful imagination.

She turned her attention to the window end of the room and ended the flirty banter that had ramped up the tingle factor in their linked hands.

She walked toward the windows, pulling Rosco with her, and stepped around a smart sitting area. A two-seater couch and two single chairs, cream with brown trim, were arranged around a glass-and-steel coffee table.

Her fingers caressed the soft folds of the curtains made of heavy cream brocade fabric, thickly cut with a modern geometric pattern, as she peeped down at the elegant street beneath them. All was serene on the cobbles below as a limousine with darkened windows purred silently away from the curb. The possibility of paparazzi lenses hidden behind those windows suddenly worried her.

She pulled back sharply, turning toward Rosco's solid chest. "This beats my industrial, exposed brick look." She smiled up at him, determined to shut out the world as the demands their linked hands were generating between them could no longer be ignored.

Rosco met her smile with smoky-blue eyes. He hooked his finger through the orange zipper loop at her collar and pulled her to him.

She joined him on a sigh as he slipped his hands beneath her coat and molded their span to her waist. They warmed her bones to melting.

"Mr. Sexy," she whispered as his mouth covered hers with a gossamer kiss. She cradled his head, entwined her fingers in his hair, pulling him closer. "More."

"Soon." He roamed away, brushing his lips along her

jawline, her cheekbone, her eyebrow.

"You could shave *one eyebrow*." She felt his smile.

"Don't tempt me."

"Too late?" he asked, the question a mischievous murmur as his lips grazed the side of her neck, then back up to her mouth. So slow. Too slow.

The sparks fizzing in her belly ignited, and she tugged his hair, demanding more.

"Too late," she whispered, and caught the soft pout of his lower lip in the kiss she'd wanted since he'd met her by the river, holding a goldfish bowl crammed full of gerberas.

The fresh, crisp fragrance of his cologne filled her senses as he kissed her back with exquisite tenderness, holding her gently against his hard body.

Gradually their kisses slowed, keeping each other from hurtling over the brink of desire, and he raised his hands to lift the length of her hair. He let it fall softly through his fingers, fanning a cool, spine-tingling breeze on the warmth of her neck.

She shuddered against him as he cupped her face. "We have something special together," he said, brushing his lips again to hers. "But I want to keep it hidden from prying lenses."

"This is all new to me." She shivered at the thought of paparazzi innuendo spoiling these magical new feelings.

He stilled, suddenly serious. "Chopper House," he said. His thumb traced her lips. "We'll go on Friday, take an early weekend." His thumb continued in another lazy circle. He dipped his head to take her mouth once more with his.

"That sounds serious," she murmured against his lips. She liked the kissing, but a weekend at his private haven? Couple territory surely. "Why do you want to go there?"

"We need some guaranteed privacy. Just a long date with no worries."

That made sense as images of cameras hidden behind

darkened city windows worried her again. "It's a date," she whispered, melding her lips with his as the feel of his mouth smothered all caution.

He smiled, looping his finger again through the orange fastener at her collar. "Bring this dress," he said, huskily Irish, against the pulse at her neck. "I've unfinished business with the zipper."

Rosco-fizzes flipped low in her abdomen as he buttoned up her coat for her. He had such a talent for wrapping her up, warm and cared for. Special.

She floated, his hand again claiming hers as they descended the stairs, and when he left her briefly to collect his coat, she picked up the bowl of gerberas, with tears misting her vision.

The glass was smooth and cool beneath her fingers, the vibrant flowers a riot of discordant color against the red of her coat. Just like her life, a mix of light and dark.

"I love the flowers," she said, hugging the bowl as Rosco rejoined her. "Thank you for today."

"My pleasure," he murmured, grazing the back of his hand down her cheek. "To be continued."

He moved to the door and peered through the security glass.

"No one outside." His tone was suddenly grim, throwing her back into reality. He opened the door, letting in the cool autumn breeze, and quickly scanned the street. "All clear. Follow me."

Kitty kept her head down just in case he was wrong. Her skin goosed creepily as the possibility of unseen eyes observing them spoiled the last of her pleasure. Going away, and into hiding, couldn't come soon enough.

• • •

The next two days were a blur as she worked to clear her calendar.

Then on Thursday morning, a bottle of award-winning red wine was delivered to her apartment.

The attached card featured a cheeky cartoon helicopter and a handwritten message:

London Heliport at 8 a.m.

Relax and sleep well, Kitty.

He'd sent her wine, a powerful message. He trusted her with alcohol. Was prepared to buy it for her.

She took a deep breath and hugged the elegantly boxed bottle to her chest. She'd take it with her, drink it with him, so to speak.

Her preparations started Thursday afternoon. She would need an early start to beat the traffic to the heliport.

Soon clothes were strewn across her bedroom, escaping out into her studio, as combinations were selected and rejected.

In the end it was a no-brainer. Her "courage" boots. Her orange zipper dress. A new silk wrap made for dancing, and anything else that made her feel her most sexy. Her usual urge to deny herself the complications of intimacy, to keep business and private life separate, were buried under the sensations Rosco aroused in her body. It was just for the weekend, she told herself. Nothing more. They'd agreed time and again neither was looking for a long-term commitment. She'd enjoy this while it lasted.

They were sure to be out of the media glare for the weekend, and Trinity St. George was not part of their shared contracts. She could take some risks.

Kitty woke early on Friday morning and drove her Citroën out of the Brick Square carpark before first light. The back of her neck prickled with anticipation as the automatic doors clanged shut behind her.

Chapter Thirteen

Rosco broke his stride as he approached the heliport carpark and watched Kitty unfold her long, elegant, boot-clad legs from her little Citroën 2CV. She leaned against the car, thumbing through her phone messages, wearing a sexy red coat cinched at her waist. Her hair, in a high ponytail, swung as she tapped her feet in the cool morning air, and his heart jack-hammered at the sight of her.

She was a picture. No wonder the media had published and re-published those photos of them together. Guilt hit him.

Double guilt. He'd gotten her into this, and now he was hiding the whole truth. His secret belief the Sandford Palace deal would require Kitty to interview with him gnawed at him. She was still vulnerable to tabloid interest. Because of him.

He cursed his lack of vigilance inviting her to such a public place and rapidly scanned the area for cameras. There were none he could see, but he hurried toward her. She looked exactly like the image he wanted to project for his business. Any crazy media attention would suit his business interests fine. But the sooner they were safely in the air and away from prying eyes, the better for her.

"Good morning, Gerbera Girl," he said, running his hand down the length of her ponytail, tugging it lightly.

"Rosco," she whispered, her voice husky as she steadied herself against his chest, one hand still holding her phone. Her body shivered in response to his touch, and he reveled in the feel of her.

"I've missed you," he murmured, and kissed her lips as soft as a ripe peach beneath his.

"Missed you, too," she murmured back.

Then they ran, laughing, to his helicopter. Rosco carrying her jam-packed camera bag and Kitty carefully balancing a large Brick Square cake tin.

He hovered protectively as she climbed into the chopper, strapped on her safety harness, and reached for the passenger headset. She knew what she was doing.

He closed the door, cocooning her from the world, and ran around the chopper to take his seat beside her. "You've flown before?"

"Twice. I had a London-from-the-air assignment." She grinned, her excitement for his own passion for flying kicking again at his heart. "Awesome views."

"The best," he agreed, and started his pre-flight procedures. She filled the cockpit with her soft floral fragrance, and he had to work hard to summon his usual focus.

Kitty gave him the thumbs-up as the headphones between them switched to live, and he returned the gesture, relishing her enthusiasm.

Then he returned his concentration to takeoff. They floated vertically with barely a lurch, leaving the helipad behind and heading for Wheatbridge Village.

Later, as the house came into view, his usual thrill was magnified by the enormity of what he was doing. He'd never brought a woman here before, but now it was hugely important that Kitty loved it. And that she felt special and safe.

The isolation and privacy of the property was one of its greatest features and even more of a plus, given their recent publicity. The thatched roof cottage, helipad, and hangar were unmistakable from the air, but nicely hidden from the road, amongst trees.

Rosco jumped down from the chopper as soon as it was safe and jogged around, bending low to take Kitty's hand as she climbed out.

He collected her bag, handed her the cake tin, and put his arm around her shoulders as they walked across the grass to the cottage. She strode beside him, looking around with obviously genuine interest, and he lowered his arm to her waist, pulling her close as they entered the small covered porch.

"Welcome."

Excitement tingled along his spine as her body responded to his. He wanted more, to hug and hold her, but without the luggage between them.

She kissed his cheek, keeping the contact between them gently bubbling as he unlocked the heavy wooden door, and he couldn't wait to show her his hideaway.

He watched her turn a slow circle as she took it all in, filling the open-plan space with her femininity. She placed her cake tin on the large farm-style table and sighed with pleasure.

"It's perfect."

She looked so contemporary amongst the ancient timber joists and white-washed walls. And yet so right. He was glad he'd trusted his instincts to bring her here.

"More gerberas." She sidestepped the sofas and bent low to touch the vase of flowers he had placed in the mullioned window overlooking the garden. "Where did you find them?"

"They're not real. There's a limit to the gerbera season, even in florist shops, I've discovered."

Kitty stayed there and looked out the tiny window. "It's all so timeless. I can imagine men and women living here through the centuries, loving and trusting each other enough to raise a family against whatever obstacles nature threw at them." She sighed, and he caught her sadness.

She turned slowly back to him and smiled. "Thank you, the flowers are a lovely thought."

"Nothing fake about the thought," he said as her golden-brown eyes met his softly across the room.

He smiled and reluctantly broke the contact. He didn't want to hurry his plans. The things he wanted to say, to do, needed to be done properly. "We have all mod-cons." Damn, he sounded like a cheery hotel proprietor. "Plenty of hot water, a shower, central heating as well as the fireplace.

"I'll show you your room." He lifted her bag and led her down a tiny hallway. "Bathroom and two bedrooms down here," he said over his shoulder. "But we've just finished a third one up in the attic."

He climbed up ladder-like steps, her heels clicking sensuously behind him, and took her into a large, coved-ceiling room, snug in the thatched eaves of the house.

Whitewashed, with heavy cotton curtains at the windows, it was furnished with character: an iron bed frame and old wicker furniture.

He placed her bag on the bed and moved to the center of the room, where the attic ceiling was just high enough for him to stand.

"It's lovely." She looked around with gratifying pleasure. "Almost like a playhouse. So charming."

"It suits you, then, Kitty. We have something special between us."

"We do." She nodded, speaking slowly.

Her cheeks flushed pink in the confined space, and the tension between them relaxed at little as he pushed his hands into the pockets of his coat and looked straight at her sparkling brown eyes.

He needed to make sure she understood him. "I do want to know you more, and you're perfectly safe with me."

"Yes." She shrugged her shoulders. "No paparazzi, anyway."

"It's our weekend, our special world. Work and the whole damn circus of life, are on hold."

"Sounds tempting. You undermine all my best business instincts, Rosco."

He knew exactly what she meant. "It's a deal, then."

"Deal," she said, a warm tide of heat smoldering in her eyes. His fists clenched as he fought the need to hold her. Time to slow down again. He steadied himself, determined to keep to his plan. He didn't want to rush.

"Tea next," he said, rubbing his hands together and grabbing hold of his hosting role with relieved gusto. "I'll get it ready while you unpack."

"Milk, no sugar, please." She waved him out of the room. "Your first new Kitty fact."

"Don't be long. We need to get out and about while the weather holds."

He clattered down the stairs, glad to escape. Kitty and a bed tucked in eaves of his cottage was a dream he couldn't have imagined a few short days ago.

A few minutes later, when Kitty joined him in the living room, he held his arms out to her and she walked straight into his hug.

Her hair was soft against his cheek and she sighed, hugging him hard. The gift of sharing this "special thing" between them was too delicious a temptation to resist.

He cradled her head, smiling lazily at her. His lips found hers. Kitty swayed against him on her heels. He held her tightly, and she took him—heart, mind, and body—straight back to the melting closeness they'd shared in his home office.

"You're warm now," he murmured. "Let me help you with your coat." She stood still for him, time meaninglessly slow, as he untied the belt of her trench.

"Just what I wanted, Rosco. You unwrapping me."

"Nothing else on my mind since I first saw you this morning."

He stepped behind her, helped her shrug out of the coat, and bent close to feather a kiss on the back of her neck. The scent and feel of her overwhelming his senses. "If I touch you again we'll never get to the next item on my list."

Kitty twisted around, found his mouth, and snatched a quick, soft kiss of her own. "Let's slow that list down a bit." She nibbled at his bottom lip, and he dived into the kind of kiss guaranteed to derail his control.

When breathing became a necessity, he forced his mouth from hers but still hugged her close, fighting the need for her. "You're too tempting for a country boy. We have some country chores to do that can't wait."

"Then we should stop." She wrenched away from him with a soft laugh, flipping her ponytail and taking her coat. "What's next?"

"Tea and cake. Keep our energy up." He strode to the kitchen, determined to control the pace of his plans.

He made the tea as Kitty tossed her coat over the sofa and opened Meg's cake tin. Rosco joined her at the table and they sat side by side, knees touching, and explored the selection of sweet treats.

Kitty chose a bite-size square of cake. "This is my favorite. Ginger spice cake wrapped in almond marzipan." She nibbled one corner and leaned closer to him, holding the treat to his lips.

He placed his hand over hers, tasted the cake with a murmur of approval, and Kitty popped the final morsel into his mouth. He licked Kitty's sweet, sticky fingers and savored the taste and feel of her so close beside him. He drew out the moment as long as he dared, then broke the contact to drain his mug of tea.

Time to move or he never would. "Let's walk. There are coats and boots in the closet for us."

"Walking is next on your list?" she said, standing and smoothing her clothes. She was wearing leggings and a tunic dress, what he was starting to think of as "Kitty-short," black and fastened at the shoulders with rows of multi-colored buttons.

He stood slowly, unable to resist touching her, and ran his fingers lightly up her arms. He rested his hands at her shoulders, his fingers toying with the smooth round buttons fastening her tunic. "You've brought such color to my life. Such a big difference in such a short time." It was true, yet unbelievable. He rubbed his cheek against hers. "I want to show you my private world. It looks best on foot."

• • •

Kitty needed to touch him again. She stretched and curled her arms around his neck. "No camera then. Just you and me."

He curved his arms at her waist, pulled her closer, hugging her hard. She hugged him back. "There's no place I'd rather be."

He took her hand and led her to the back porch. She giggled as her feet swam in a pair of Wellington boots several sizes too big and already encrusted with mud. "Instant farm girl."

Rosco helped her into a padded jacket that reached down over the top of the boots. She laughed again, dangling the sleeves well beyond her hands. "No need for gloves."

She rolled up the sleeves and waited while he put on his

own boots and coat then slung a small rucksack over one shoulder.

"Chopper first." He grabbed her hand. "We need to secure it for the night. Easiest now before it rains."

Kitty stumbled across the grass beside him, adjusting her stride as her feet slipped in her boots. He looked so different out of his crisp city clothes—a different kind of competent—but still Rosco.

She loved this version of him, manly in jeans and hunting jacket. And sexy.

She hoped Rosco couldn't read her mind. Because the only thing she'd wanted since he'd tugged her ponytail hello was to be in his arms. His hands on her body. His lips kissing hers.

He made light work of jacking up the chopper and pulling it into the hangar. They clanged the doors shut together, and he grabbed her hand again.

"What's next?"

"A landlordly walk around the boundaries." He grinned and puffed out his chest. "We've eleven acres."

It was pretty land, green and gently undulating. Kitty stopped to admire one view across the countryside to a picture-book village, complete with church spire. "This is my favorite spot, the main reason I bought the property."

He veered away from the perimeter fence, steering her toward some trees. "I thought we could have lunch in the woods." It was a slightly grandiose description for a small stand of trees, and she laughed with him as she followed him along a rough, well-worn path into a small clearing.

She shivered against a sudden feeling of entrapment. This would be a perfect place for paparazzi to hide. She placed her hand on Rosco's back to rid herself of the idea of being watched. The whole reason he'd chosen Chopper House for their date was because of how out of the way it was. And surely the paps had to be on to some new prey now.

The path eventually led to an old but comfortable-looking wooden bench, and they sat together with a sigh, Kitty falling with an ungainly Michelin Man-like bounce in her oversized jacket.

Rosco steadied her with a grin and opened the rucksack at his feet to produce a quick picnic. "Sandwiches and Coke for me. Muesli and red wine for you."

He opened the small bottle of wine and handed it to her. "Chocolate coated," he said, then tore the wrapper off the muesli bar.

The trees encircled them with the air of an outdoor chapel, rich with earthy green aromas and only birdsong for company. She sat in silence, wine in one hand, muesli bar in the other, and watched Rosco as he chomped into his sandwich.

He looked like a man eating with purpose, fueling his energy, his gaze momentarily far away.

She sipped her wine, her fluttering tummy telling her she was going to need it. "Death," she said with certainty. "Our parents' deaths. They're next on your list."

Her body shrank farther inside her coat as she searched her heart for the extra courage she needed, sensing Rosco was struggling with the same challenge.

"Our under-the-table oath," he said, his voice quiet and firm. "The same oath counts in this place. It's as private as I've got, and you're free to walk away whenever you want."

He reached into his coat pocket, pulled out a bunch of keys, and placed them on the seat between them. "My house and car keys. Your escape at any time. I can chopper back to London on my own."

Kitty nodded, left them untouched. "Just you and me," she whispered, tussling with trust and truth. "Kiss me," she said.

"My pleasure." His voice warmed with the hint of a smile.

She lifted her hands up and away from her face, still holding the wine and food. She was suddenly breathless at the tenderness in his eyes.

"Muesli again," he said, his murmur a soft caress as he thumbed her chin, then kissed her lips. Lingering, caring, and questioning.

"Suicide," she whispered. "Don't move. Kiss me again."

His lips stayed on hers, soft, soothing the knots twisting her heart. "My Kitty," he said, pulling very slightly away, slowly running his hand through her hair.

She rested her hands on her lap with a sigh, steadying the wine and lulled by the rhythm of his fingers in her hair.

"Jacqueline killed herself. Drugs and alcohol. I bolted out of the funeral. It made the papers. Just one short splash of newspaper headlines; thank goodness, she was an out-of-date model by then. I left school as soon as I could." She swallowed, the story somehow stuck in her throat. "Shock and shame."

"Hell, Kitty. Did she die in her house? The one like mine?" His hand stilled in her hair, his eyes stricken and dark.

"No," she assured him. The relief was plain on his face. "She chose a little hotel in Scotland." She needed to get her story out. To finish it. "It's demolished now, part of a new motorway extension. All gone." She sipped her wine. "That's who I am. An unwanted child. The daughter of a suicide statistic. I hated her." The hurt of that hate stabbed, suddenly fierce in her memory.

"You were a child. You deserved so much more."

"I grew strong on my own. I was safe on my own. Family skills aren't part of my inheritance." Another sip of wine helped dull the bitterness. "Two years at art college, courtesy of my absent father's education fund. Then I was gone—overseas until Ralph talked me into returning to England."

She bent down, put her mini-bottle of wine on the ground. "A few years later and it would still be all over the internet—

that's my only positive."

"Mine, too," he said, clasping her hand, pulling it into his lap. "I can't imagine how much worse that would make it."

He took a breath, waited a beat. "I was with him when he died." His voice was low and hard and Kitty squeezed his hand, suddenly goose-pimpled with distress for the fourteen-year-old Rosco having to witness his father's death.

"I've never been allowed to forget it. I've never been alone and *able* to forget it." He flexed his right leg beside her, stretching it out in front of him, his thigh just touching hers.

"I've lived ever since with expectations." He turned slightly toward her, his gaze faraway. "The family's expectations that I revere his memory." Bitter. His tone, so bitter. "My expectations of myself, to protect my mother from worry and grief. She'd suffered enough and there were three of us to care for and a business to run."

Kitty's heart clenched, and she leaned forward, kissed his cheek, returning his tenderness. "He was driving drunk. Showing off in his new car. I said he shouldn't drive, but he laughed at me." Rosco shook his head at the memory. "I thought if he made a mistake I could grab the wheel, keep us on track."

Kitty held her breath. Waited with dread.

"He crossed the center line. He drove into an oncoming car. Both drivers dead at the scene. I was flung to the side, just my knee and thigh in the line of impact."

"Rosco," she whispered, her hand moving softly to his thigh. "Were you knocked unconscious?"

"My mother thought I was. But I remember it all. That smack of metal, the smell of oil, my father slumped over the tangled wheel. Violent, then surreally quiet until the sirens came."

"Were you in pain?" How frightening, just a boy and all alone until help arrived.

"I don't remember pain at the time."

His bleak profile twisted Kitty's heart. She slipped her feet out of the cold rubber of her Wellington boots and snuggled up to Rosco, hugging him close on the hard wooden bench.

He returned the hug, wrapping his arms around her, accepting her comfort.

"Two operations. I was tied to tubes and on morphine when the funeral was held." He rubbed his cheek against her hair. "So glad I missed the funeral." Bitter again.

Kitty nodded against his chest. "You don't need to explain that to me." She heaved a sigh on his behalf. "Just fill in the gaps about your leg. I want to understand."

"Knee smashed. Muscles above the knee badly torn," he said, still holding her tight. "I've had two knee replacements. The muscle rehab was the worst. Painful for years."

"School must have been hard."

"No more sport. Except swimming, but I only did that at the rehab pool. I didn't want anyone to see how ugly my leg looked. To have to talk about it. And girls didn't think much of a guy who couldn't dance."

"Girls," she said, clucking her tongue, mocking gently. "A real woman appreciates a good sexy sway to a slow tune." She shifted slightly, placed her cheek against his. "You've got that nailed."

Chapter Fourteen

Rosco felt the heaviness of the past leaving him slowly. The warmth of the woman in his arms stirring him to action.

He smiled as they held each other, all talked out, in the peace of their sheltered retreat. "What do you want to do next?"

"Find some junk food. Burgers oozing with cheese. Ice cream dripping with chocolate sauce," she said, moving away from him. "Retail therapy in the village. What do you think?"

"You're a woman of surprises." He'd said it mildly as he pulled her back against his body, but he didn't want to share her with the world today. There was something discordant about her sudden need to shop, of all things. To leave their private haven and let the world in.

He remembered her words. *That's me. An unwanted child.* He hated the feeling of rejection behind those words. If she was testing him in some way. Or giving him the opportunity to step away from her. She needed to know her mother's suicide only made him admire and want her even more.

"I think you deserve whatever you want. For me, the

shops can wait. The village will always be there." He rested his cheek against the softness of her hair and felt her stiffen slightly. "I want you to myself right now." He nuzzled her neck, thrilled as she softened against him.

"Shopping isn't your thing, then?" she murmured, and he felt her smile against his cheek.

"No." He moved, pulling her onto his knee. "I thought we might move to more private… activities."

Her arms circled his neck, her dark eyes sparkling wickedly at his. She couldn't fail to read how much he wanted her. Just her.

"I think I'm with you," she said, and swiveled to sit astride his thighs.

The past was completely gone for him; now he was lost in the feel of her against him.

His body clenched with need for her. "Home?" he asked, linking his fingers through hers, taking the weight of her body as she swayed toward him.

She nodded. She wanted him, too. He fought for restraint. "Just a wee bit of kissing in the woods and then back to my list?" he teased. He tugged her forward and kissed her, her response hot and instant. She tasted of wine and chocolate as she wriggled in his lap, spurring him on.

"Wouldn't want to spoil your tick list," she said, her breath warm against his mouth. She grinned, impish with pleasure, and began unbuttoning his jacket, then hers. And then there were just light woolen layers between them, the long curvy line of her waist, the soft rise of her breasts, his to hold.

"I'll not be undressing you in the cold." He amped up his Irishness, watched her pupils dilate for him. "But I'm not leaving the woods without kissing you properly."

He leaned in close, kissed her mouth, hungry beneath his, and shuddered as she slipped her hands inside his jacket.

Then he took control.

His hands started at her waist, caressing the line of her body, so slow, until she whimpered for more. Then he deepened his kiss, meeting her need with his, first soft and sensual, then hot and urgent, everything else forgotten.

Until the first drops of rain drove them apart.

• • •

Kitty twisted away from Rosco, his kiss still hot on her lips. She picked up his keys and dropped them into his hand. "I won't be needing these."

As he returned them to his coat pocket, she scrambled off his lap and then they ran across the paddocks to the cottage. Breathless and wet, they tumbled into the warmth.

Rosco immediately snagged her body back to his. "My list continues." He kissed her so hot she fancied steam rose between their damp clothes.

"What's next?" She knew what she wanted from him.

"A hot, hot shower." He grinned at her, teasing.

"You think I need heating up?" She quirked a brow at him, matching his grin.

"You know I don't." He leaned in to touch his nose to hers, and a flush of lust surged through her veins.

She stilled in his arms, images of showering with Rosco filling her mind.

"There's a hamper of goodies in the bathroom." His whisper tickled her cheek. "Enjoy the luxury, and I'll join you in a few minutes."

"You're a details man."

"Certainly am." He stroked her earlobe, slow and tender, and his intensity buzzed around her heart.

It was a wrench to leave him, even for a few minutes, but preparing to be loved by Rosco Redmond was worth taking time over.

She had to stop herself from doing an unladylike skip as she headed for the shower.

The hamper was a rustic basket full to tumbling with thick, soft towels, scented soaps, and creamy lotions. A beeswax candle and a box of long matches were nestled on top of the towels.

He had thought of everything.

Slowly, to draw out the pleasure of anticipation, she placed the candle safely away from towels and struck a match. It flared bright, the faintly acrid smell of the burning matchhead chasing a shiver of danger down her spine.

Then temptation spurred her into action, wanting to be ready for Rosco. She turned on the shower, peeled off her clothes, and selected a plush white towel to wrap around her body.

As steam filled the room, she selected a jar of silky lotion, twisted the top to release the sweet fragrance of jasmine, and smoothed some over her arms and throat.

The scent was heavenly and, as it mingled with the steam, she felt enveloped in luxury and desire.

She lifted her hair and twisted it into a knot, securing it with a bright orange clip conveniently clinging to the basket edge. A Rosco detail just for her.

Dreamy, she released the towel, selected pure white soap, and stepped into the shower.

As the water warmed her skin, Rosco joined her.

"Beautiful Kitty," he said on a murmur as he bent his lips to her neck. Her body buzzed again at his feathery kiss.

Then his mouth met hers with hunger and tenderness. Lips soft and giving, tongues dancing and demanding, as the steam swirled around them.

Mutual passion spurred them on, aching to touch and to pleasure.

Rosco pulled back, ran his hands down the sides of her

body, circled her wrists, then caressed the length of her bare arms with his fingertips.

Kitty shuddered at his touch, ran her hands up his arms, relishing the hard, sinewy feel of him—the strength of golden skin over muscle.

He stroked her face, her hands still holding his arms, then kissed her again, long, slow, and wanting.

Then he inhaled softly, his warm, soft lips moving to the swell of her breasts. Intent, he gave his full attention to each soft curve in turn. Slowly, he raised desire-dark eyes to hers and kissed her lips again with the sensual pull of unhurried tenderness.

Kitty moved her hand to cradle his head, lacing her fingers through the springy brown waves of his hair as he lowered his lips to nestle between her breasts where the water slicked her skin.

Then he dragged his mouth back to hers. "All right, my Kitty?" he murmured against her lips, as drugged as she was by their mutual desire.

She nodded, smiling dreamily into his dark blue eyes, unable to find her voice to speak.

Time stopped for her. She was lost in his touch.

"My turn," she said on a ragged breath, moving her hands up over his chest where the hard feel of him left her wanting more. She licked the trickles of water from his chest and claimed him for her own.

She fought her melting craving for him, slowing her pace to match his, taking her time to touch, to caress his athlete-smooth torso. The flat, hard muscles; broad, firm chest; strong shoulders and back.

She followed her hands with her lips, stoking her desire. He shuddered, cupping one hand at her neck, and when she was ready, dragged her mouth back to his.

"My beautiful Kitty," he murmured again. Her breath

caught in her throat, and she swayed against him, soft with longing. His hands followed her need, resting warm and seductive at the dip of her waist.

"Would you be wanting more?" he asked, lifting his head to look into her eyes.

"Yes," she heard herself say, her voice barely more than a whisper, her hand weightless as she captured the sexy pout of his lower lip with her thumb.

"Then we should be finding my bed." He smiled, those smoky-blue eyes locking with hers as he reached for a towel. He turned off the water, wrapped her, tenderly securing the towel at her breast, and lifted her into his arms.

Kitty felt like she was floating as he nudged the bedroom door open with his foot and kicked it closed behind them, his eyes never leaving her face.

He gently set her on her feet beside the lit fire for warmth. "Don't move," he whispered.

Kitty nodded, dazed with her need for him as the fire flickered golden over his bare, muscled chest. And, she stood, mesmerized, as he tugged the towel from her body.

Then they were naked again, and his first touch at her waist goosed her flesh in that unique cold-hot Rosco fizz. She heard herself whimper as his hands and mouth explored her flesh and roused her beyond feeling. She barely registered the moment he lifted her again before lowering her to his soft, warm bed.

His hands continued to caress and arouse, his mouth teasing hers, unrelenting, as she melted and quivered in a world that held only him, hot in the glow of the fire.

Much later, Kitty stretched dreamy and content beneath Rosco's sheets.

He stirred beside her and smiled, met her mouth with a sweet, lazy kiss.

"Are you all right, Kitty?"

She ran the back of her fingers down the now stubbled angle of his jaw. "Yes," she said, amazed at how easily he'd swept her away. She felt like someone else. Someone abandoned on a sea of emotion.

He scooped her body to his. "Good," he murmured against her hair. "Because we haven't finished my list of simple country pleasures yet."

"Sexy list maker," she purred as his hands roamed the length of her body.

He rolled her onto her back, raised her arms above her head, and she stretched beneath him.

"Is there anything you want to add to the list?"

"More," she said. "Just more of our world, all night, all morning."

"More." He rolled the word on his tongue. "That's on my list, too." He smiled, his hands circling her wrists, his mouth soft on hers.

"Details," he said. "We know a good list does need details. I have food, and dancing naked by the fire, on mine."

"You've advanced your dancing skills to naked already?"

"I've always been a fast learner," he said. "Tell me what you want, Kitty."

She sighed beneath him, moved her hands to his hair and down over the smooth skin of his back.

"Unwrapping. You're so good at unwrapping me." Unwrapping her heart. It was a scary first. No other man had tempted the story of her mother's suicide from her. No other man had seared through her reserve to earn this degree of closeness.

But when he lifted his head to smile into her eyes, his passion quenched the tide of caution threatening to analyze her pleasure.

The warm burr of his voice flowed over her as his hands continued their lazy caress. "It's a skill I'm keen to further improve."

She imagined wearing her silk wrap dress for him later, could already feel the soft fabric on her bare skin and the release of Rosco undoing the leather tie. That would be for later. For now, she had other plans.

"Seduce me again," she asked, stretching beneath him. "I want *you* on my list."

The next day, as late-morning light filtered through the still-closed curtains, they sat in bed with Meg's cake tin between them, drinking mugs of hot tea.

"Pumpkin reality in thirty minutes, Cinders." Rosco clinked his china mug to hers. "I promised to get you back in time for your meeting."

"Don't mention it yet," she groaned. "Brick Square, Jabbering Gerbera, media rubbish, work and responsibilities. I left them all at home, and now they're crowding back on me." She gulped a hot mouthful of tea, washed the thoughts from her mind. It wasn't yet time to question.

"So, shhh..." She placed her finger against his soft, warm mouth. "Thirty more minutes of Rosco-Kitty world."

She selected a square of caramel fudge from the tin, took a bite, felt the sweetness dissolve in her mouth. Then, raising the remaining half to Rosco's mouth, she traced his sexy lower lip with the sugary treat.

"Temptation." He grinned, deliciously wolfish, and took the caramel into his mouth, sucking her fingers and waggling his brows.

"Irresistible temptation," she agreed, stretching across him and placing their mugs on the nightstand.

Her body wanted him again, and she turned to sit astride him, tenting the thick, soft covers around them.

"Last on my list," she said as she faced him, skin to skin. "One more kiss."

He took her mouth, sharing the lingering sweet flavor of caramel, and scooped her body to his one last time.

Those last thirty minutes sped by in a blur, and all to soon Kitty laid her head on his shoulder as sadness washed over her. "No more time for passion."

He rubbed his cheek against her hair. "It's our world to step back into whenever we want. Our oath and passion will be waiting for us."

"Already on my tick list," she said, snuggling her head to his chest, hiding the doubts she felt surely must be showing on her face. It was the real world that bothered her now.

A new worry floated across her thoughts like random dust on a camera lens, spoiling the image. Would Rosco still want her back in the real world? He hadn't wanted to take her to the village.

Did not wanting to share her really mean he was ashamed to be in public with her?

When they did return to normal life she would need to find out.

• • •

"Three, two, one," they counted together at noon, and Rosco blinked as he switched on his cell phone. The screen lit up with unread messages blasting him back to reality.

At the top of the list was a message bearing the Sandford Palace coat of arms.

He clicked it open and groaned aloud as an ornate invitation filled the screen. It set out a time for him and his "mystery woman" to attend an interview high tea.

Kitty noticed his annoyance and flicked a look at the screen before he could jab it closed.

"Huh," she snorted, snatching the phone from him and devouring the invite information. "Trinity St. George! There's no way she wants to meet me."

Rosco absorbed Kitty's self-scorn and felt the acid burn of unfairness. Kitty was nothing like these people. They had no right to judge her.

"Why do you single out Trinity St. George?" He'd hoped to avoid involving Kitty in this ridiculous situation. People he hardly knew shouldn't dictate his private life.

Kitty turned to him but didn't meet his eyes. "She was a friend of my mother's, but they were very competitive. Trinity abandoned my mother to marry the duke."

"Why didn't you tell me?" Anger and betrayal smacked through him, and he drew away from her, hauling in his temper. "I would have understood," he insisted, unable to hide the hurt he was feeling. After all, it was one of his father's enemies who had put them in this situation.

Kitty drew breath and scrunched farther into the folds of the bedding. "You told me I would have nothing to do with them." She visibly cringed. "Is that meeting what this weekend was about? You thought if you seduced me I would go with you to your meeting?" She was on the verge of tears now, and Rosco was helpless to stop her. "You plotted wrong, I'm afraid," she scoffed angrily. "Trinity won't want me haunting her from the past and threatening her aristocratic image."

"That's not at all why I brought you to Chopper House—you know that." He couldn't control the bite in his tone, cursed himself as she rounded on him.

"Do I?" she spat at him. "You manipulated me." She tossed his phone back at him, and he flinched at her words.

It hadn't felt like manipulation to him. He'd let go. Let their mutual attraction seduce him away from business, against all his instincts. Against everything his father had unwittingly taught him.

Against his own better judgment.

He'd wanted to escape business, but Kitty's past made that impossible. The closer they had grown, the bigger the divide between them over the palace deal. Now he had no interview prospects with her.

And much worse, Kitty no longer trusted him. Not at all where he had intended to end their weekend.

He punched the pillow in frustration and turned to comfort her distress.

• • •

Kitty clenched her fist around her cell phone, clutching it to her chest, and launched herself out of bed in the half light. "I've had enough talk." Rosco's anger and her sense of betrayal were too much to stomach any longer.

She was naked and grabbed a shirt Rosco had discarded sometime during the night.

Its soft cotton, rumpled with Rosco-ness, irritated her now as she slipped it over her skin and secured a couple of buttons.

Stretching aching muscles, she stepped purposefully away from him to the window by the bed where the soft midday light, filtering through thick brown fabric, offered a gentle re-entry into the world.

She pulled the curtains aside and *screamed.*

Yanking the curtains back across the window, she ran around the bed, heading for the door. "Tele lens the size of a dinner plate," she hissed, picking up her cell phone, fury propelling her across the room.

Rosco instantly bounded out of bed to intercept her, but she sidestepped him.

"Get dressed," she said, pushing him away and running to the front door, not wanting to be stopped by him or to lose sight of the paparazzo It was the guy with the squashy face, and she'd had enough.

"Stop, Kitty," she heard Rosco call behind her, and it made her run faster.

Her bare feet hit the wooden porch, the concrete driveway, and then she was dimly aware of softer damp grass as she accelerated toward her target. He was running towards the road.

School athletics training kicked in and she planted her feet, toes up, to maximize glute power and drove her arms back hard to boost her speed.

She'd catch the creep and get his camera off him if it killed her.

Gaining on him was easy. He was stumbling, obviously torn between escape and protecting his camera and the photos he'd snatched.

Kitty wanted to yell her head off at him but saved her breath for the sprint

A green car, half hidden in bushes at the edge of the country road, came into view. She'd swear it was the one she'd imagined was following her to the wedding. The one she'd lost sight of and dismissed as fanciful. She should have trusted her gut.

Panting, she finally caught up with him as he wrenched open his car door and dived in. She threw herself at that door just as he clicked it locked.

"You low life, creepzoid," she shouted, aiming her phone camera at him. "I've got your face now and your plate number."

"It's a rental, Kitty Mayfair," he sneered through the car window, gunning the engine.

A cold tide of fear swept through her.

He knew her name.

Her carefully constructed adult life flashed in front of

her eyes. The truth about her mother's suicide, all the ancient titillating gossip about her childhood, could pop up in some psycho-babble article alongside this guy's bedroom shot.

He'd publish it all for a few hundred bucks and a laugh in the pub.

Her privacy would also be lost, her reputation tainted along with Rosco's. She felt the icy claw of lost love freeze any hope that what they'd shared had been real.

Rosco skidded to a halt beside her, wearing only shoes and boxer shorts, and he hit the car door with force. But the guy just laughed as he squealed away from them. Taking her hopes with him.

Rosco had misled her about Trinity St. George, and now the paparazzi had enough snaps and info to ruin her.

Chapter Fifteen

Breathing hard, Rosco caught Kitty around the waist. She was amped up and ready to take off after the car as it disappeared around the bend in the road.

Her heart pounded beneath his hands as she kicked his shins, struggling to escape. He held her closer, his temper seething next to hers. Their privacy breached.

"He's gone," he said, waiting for her adrenalin surge to fade.

"I want to find him, destroy his camera." Kitty's voice was taut, her breath hot against his skin.

"I knew this was all too good to be true," she said, using her fists to pummel his arms.

His own adrenalin rush turned clammy-cold at her tone. Then anger at himself, and at the damn paps, raged through him again. He was the one who'd been selfish enough to think he could carve out some happiness without consequences. He had deliberately tuned out his childhood lessons, and this was the cost.

Kitty continued to wriggle, and he held on tight. He was

afraid for her hurt, for this cruel ending to their weekend.

"I should never have opened that curtain."

"To be sure, it's a crime for a beautiful woman to draw a curtain in her own bedroom." He turned on the brogue in the hope she'd laugh and melt his fear.

But she stilled in his arms with no answering banter. "It isn't *my* bedroom. That's the story."

"It is your bedroom in our world, Gerbera Girl. No one else's."

"That's still the story," she repeated, and pulled away from him. "I've brought the paparazzi to your door."

The adrenalin was gone, but he refused to let their world fade with it. "You know that isn't true. *I* know that isn't true."

"They 'arrived' with me for that first pre-wedding photo shoot. *Your words*, Rosco," she said as he turned her toward him, his heart squeezing at the sight of her hurt, pinched face. "You blamed me then," she persisted. "And you've never trusted me since."

Kitty started to shiver in his arms, and it wrung his heart even as his brain kicked into action mode. He propelled her back toward the house, acutely aware of the cold air on his bare chest and her bare feet on the damp grass.

He kept his arm clamped around her waist, scared she would take off without listening to him. "I'm sorry I put you in this situation."

When they reached the porch he cupped her trembling chin, ensuring she paid attention. "I told you when we met at Brick Square that an old business enemy of my father's is stalking me. He'll be paying that guy to snoop and snap me to undermine my reputation. He wants to destroy my bid for the Sandford Palace contract."

"That makes it worse." She shrugged off his embrace. "They're hunting me, too. They could be anywhere in the trees. Even yesterday…" She looked around wild-eyed and suspicious.

"He wouldn't have been lurking outside if he'd got the pictures he wanted yesterday."

"At least I was fully clothed yesterday." She wrapped her arms around her waist and he ached to hold her again, as much for his own comfort as hers.

He'd failed in protecting her. In making their world safe and private. In gaining her trust.

When they stepped inside the house, she was pale and trembling, looking as bleak as his own reflection in the bathroom mirror as he turned on the shower and insisted she defrost under the hot water.

No steamy loving this time. He felt the loss as he rushed to make sweet tea and collect the last of her Brick Square cakes. He wanted to pull her out of her shock. They couldn't escape this intrusion and he'd do what was needed to get it in perspective now.

He heard the shower turn off and dragged the velvet comforter from his bed to wrap her up warm. She still looked a little wild-eyed as she emerged from the steam, and he pulled her gently into the living room.

"I've made tea," he said as she hunched in the corner of the sofa, tapping at her cell phone. Surely she wouldn't find any of those wretched photos online this soon. "We'll stay hidden a little longer."

"Not ashamed of me, of my history, are you?" Her voice was bitter, her scorn turned inward as she snapped her phone closed. "The real world is just a short car ride away. Even worse, just an instant click on the internet. That's where you'll find me now."

"Of course I'm not ashamed."

He moved closer, reached for her hand, but she snatched it away. "None of this"—she waved her hand around the room—"weekend was real."

"It is. It's special. Sandford Palace meeting or not, what we shared here was real."

"Even if it was, that creepzoid's wrecked it. We'll be all over the internet, and your mystery woman will hardly have the reputation you want."

"We don't know that. The creepzoid's photos—great name, by the way, although I can think of others. His photos will be unusable," he said, grappling for positives. "He was a long way from the window."

"They'll do. He'll enhance them. The quality won't matter because he has what he wants." She pulled the comforter up over her head, burrowing farther away from him. "He knows my name." Anger surged within him as he watched her profile harden, her gaze inward and self-destructive. "He's older than most paps—he must have been around when my mother died. Must have remembered who I am." She twisted to face him. "Your double bad luck, Rosco."

"Rubbish." He reached out to comfort her, but she flinched away. "I'm leaving the country tomorrow. You can negotiate the Brick Square contract with Rosa. I'll start the photography when I get back."

He heaved in a furious breath and glared at her. "You're making no sense. Where the hell are you going?"

"One of those travel assignments I told you about was confirmed. I emailed back to accept while I was in the bathroom."

"How long for?"

"Three weeks."

Her brown eyes swam with unshed tears, and he couldn't ignore her pain. Hell, it was his pain, too. "You're running away from us."

"No. I'm setting us free from hiding and innuendo."

"We can't let others do this to us. We can still have our own world." God, he wanted to hold her. He reached out again to touch her, to ease the pain, but she batted him away.

"It isn't about others. It's about us." Her voice was a tear-choked rasp against his heart. "It's about me."

Fear clenched through him, and he braced his body against the sofa. "What *about* you?" He snatched a glance at her. Couldn't bear to watch the rigid stubborn lines of her rejection.

Kitty took a shuddering breath, then talked in a rush. "Family. I don't know how to do family the way you do behind your smart London door. Those skills just aren't in my DNA. I've jinxed yours already."

She sniffed, drew in another ragged breath. "So whatever this 'special thing' is we have, it's over. It will always be tainted by paparazzi now. It always has been. You only want me when we're hidden away, Rosco."

Tears caught at her throat, and she swallowed then continued, her voice thick and fierce, as dread filled him. "Special in our own world means secret, hidden. I can't see a way ahead for that."

"What do you mean by 'a way ahead'?"

"No future. Perhaps I'm Jacqueline Mayfair's daughter after all, in more ways than I've dared to think."

"You're talking rubbish again." She made no sense. She was nothing like her mother.

"Really, Rosco? Let me spell it out." She shifted to face him squarely. "I wanted a job and a contract. I wanted to stand up against your bullying family and the media. Then I wanted more…too much more."

She breathed heavily again, shuddering. "Our under-the-tablecloth and Chopper House worlds aren't real. They're not sustainable against all this. I should never have trusted temptation. Now I'm hurting you. It's the last thing I want to do."

Kitty planted her feet on the floor, pulling herself up and

away from him. "I need to go home. Think this through."

He eyed her determined stance and rubbed an exasperated hand across his jaw. Everything he'd worked for seemed turned against him.

He needed to think, too.

"Get your things together. I'll fly you back to London."

She fled upstairs without comment, and he switched his concentration onto preparing the chopper, planning the flight. Tasks that didn't require him to search his soul the way the bleak look on Kitty's face did.

• • •

The helicopter cockpit felt like a glass cage as he flew a silent Kitty back to London. It was the first time since gaining his license that his spirits hadn't lifted with the chopper.

Kitty feigned sleep, and he left her alone. The emotions he was keeping under close control were incompatible with safe flying.

When they landed she stirred immediately, unbuckled her harness, and reached for the cockpit door.

"Don't rush away. We can work this out."

"No." She shook her head, emphatic, distress in every line of her body. "Those photos will be out there now."

"Nonsense." Surely they wouldn't be plastered all over the media already. Hopefully never.

"Get your cell phone. It will be posted for everyone to see now. Even your Trinity St. George."

He stilled as he dug into the pocket of his jeans to grab his phone, activated it, and handed it to Kitty.

"You'll find them quicker than me." He crossed his fingers, hoping she was wrong, sure that she was. This was crazy.

The look on her face told him the worst, and he leaned closer, watching with her, as images of them filled the small screen.

Kitty and him beside her little car at the heliport. She leaning into him, on her toes in her high-heeled boots, as his hand caressed the length of her pony tail.

Anger swelled, a physical pressure in his chest.

Kitty at full stretch opening their bedroom curtains, with him, clearly bare chested, in the bed behind her.

Desperate, he urged her to scroll to the end of the article. "No photos of us in the woods," he said, his voice a croak he couldn't control.

"There's more," she said, scrolling intently down the screen. "The text is the worst."

LOVERS HEAL TOGETHER. The title curdled his blood.

The publisher and the photographer overcome alcohol- and suicide-devastated childhoods in each other's arms.

Their businesses were named, James's and Jacqueline's deaths inaccurately dated and described, followed by a very short quote from some unknown shrink about childhood damage affecting adult relationships.

"The final humiliation," she said. "They looked back and found our secrets."

"And twisted them together." He'd used everything in his power to control his public life. To protect his family's reputation.

"I'll get my legal team on it and fight this. It's all rubbish—the wedding, Titania, and the palace contract saga."

"They're red herrings," she said, her voice sad and flat. "The real story is you."

"I've always been discreet. Under the radar."

"That's my point. You don't need me in your public life."

She threw his phone in his lap and wrenched open the cabin door, tumbling down the steps, away from him. She was already opening the cargo hatch as he dived out of his side of the cabin after her. He retrieved her bag, and she snatched it from him. "I can't do this."

He took hold of her arm, forcing her to stop. Her eyes were wet and huge in her pale face, wild with emotion that seemed illogical to him. Overwrought.

Yet it was passion he knew he couldn't bear to lose now that he'd found it.

He looked her square in the eye. "You need to know, Kitty, that I don't give up on what I want."

He watched her pupils dilate then glaze over with cynicism. He hated to see it. To cause it. "All right, go for now." He softened his tone, let go of her arm. "I don't want you to suffer anymore. I'll call you when I've sorted it."

"You can't sort it. You can't change the past or the tabloids."

He threw himself back into the chopper and watched her walk away from him, hurrying to her car. Her usual sway was clipped and stiff, the cake tin clutched under her arm, a poignant symbol of the sweetness lost between them.

• • •

Kitty let the tears flow as she crept along with the end-of-day London traffic. She sniffed and swiped her wet cheeks and couldn't wait to get to Brick Square.

It was a first for her—having a place to run back to.

Exhausted, she dragged her bag out of the car and collapsed into the private lift as her Sisterhood phone rocked out its demanding anthem.

"Kitty, where are you? Rosco Redmond's just emailed me, saying he's worried about you getting home safely," said Rosa with her usual blend of concern and efficiency.

Kitty rolled her eyes. "The man's a control freak. I'm fine."

"He sounded concerned, not controlling. Where are you?"

"Just walking out of the lift."

"Go straight to the living room," ordered Rosa's soft firm voice.

"I want to be alone."

"You can be later. We're all on our way."

Rosa rang off, and Kitty dragged her sad, sorry self to do as she was told. No matter how bad things got, the Sisterhood had sworn to support each other. Their bond was elastic enough for individuality but precious enough never to be compromised.

There was no escape from a complete explanation and everyone's corresponding full support.

An hour later, Kitty was propped up on a sofa, wrapped in a throw, surrounded by comfy cushions and her concerned, caring half sisters.

"That's the end of my rant." She toyed with the fringe of the throw, an impossibly girly pink compared to the soft but practical brown comforter at Chopper House.

There was so much more than the facts to her feelings for Rosco. Through no fault of his own, his history and position in life were a threat to her privacy. And she to his.

What a tangle. The sense of self she'd grown so painstakingly since she was sixteen had been compromised for a man. How like her mother was that?

"I'm sorry I've mixed business with pleasure and caused all this drama. Me, of all people."

"About time," said Danni. "We're not the nunnery kind of sisterhood."

"Rosco *is* exceptional," said Tessa, grinning at Danni. "Since you've been working with him, I've suddenly heard his name everywhere. Sport and charity fundraiser. He's hot, too, let me say before Danni beats me to rating him."

"If you're going to mix business with pleasure he's a smart choice," Rosa agreed, patting Kitty's knee. "You can see him again when you're ready."

"I'll never be ready," she said. "He deceived me. Hid the full threat of Trinity St. George from me." She'd trusted him, and he'd let her down. "What a nightmare."

"It will look more positive with time. The tabloid interest will stop," Rosa said decisively. "You simply aren't important or famous enough to be in the spotlight any longer."

"Thanks." Sisterly love had a bite today. But it helped to talk, to have support.

Rosa smiled softly. "Your work will go on, and Rosco will be businesslike, considerate, I'm sure."

"I promised to work with him. I don't want to jeopordize the Brick Square project for all of you."

"Sounds like a continued connection to me," Rosa said, looking at the others for support.

"Yes, it does," agreed Tessa. "Your hurt seems to be caused by the paparazzi, not Rosco."

"It's all the same thing," Kitty said, wishing she could explain the tangle of emotions. "If I didn't have a history, none of it would have happened. I'd be able to handle *his* being in the tabloids if I didn't have so much to hide."

"The revelations aren't your fault," Tessa said. "It's assault by tabloid insinuation."

"Yes. Almost like blackmail," Kitty agreed. "But it all started when I turned up on his doorstep." She wrung her hands at the memory. "I wish I'd never taken that contract."

"Nonsense," said Rosa, business brusque. "You did that for sound professional reasons, and then for Rosco's sister. You gave them the wedding album they wanted."

"It seems so long ago."

"That's because you've invested your feelings in Rosco, not in his family," said Danni.

"I don't do family. I told him that."

"You've got us and you're doing just fine."

"That's what he said."

"Then he got to know you well." Danni quirked her eyebrow. "Powerful stuff. To be understood. To be whisked away by helicopter and romanced."

"Yes, like a fairy tale." Too late, she heard the little-girl longing in her own voice. The scared ten-year-old, the orphaned teenager who'd roamed the world to avoid making a home, or trusting love to build a family.

She'd wanted this fairy tale to be true. Wanted this happily-ever-after she'd never believed she was special enough to deserve.

"I'm confused," she confessed. She felt duped by his withholding the potential meeting with Trinity St. George. Yet the smile in his voice, the warmth in his kisses, and the passion in his loving had seemed so real. He couldn't have faked it all. Could he?

"Your thoughts are fogged with emotion and you're hyped," Danni continued. "Getting away and working it off is a good idea. In the end, you'll need to be honest with yourself and settle it with Rosco."

"Just come back," said Meg, giving Kitty a quick hug.

• • •

The tour bus company picked Kitty up at seven the next morning. Relief washed over her as she slipped into a seat and the bus drove off. The relief of leaving everyone behind and of getting away without Rosco Redmond's interference.

The anger in his voice and that now familiar clenched jaw worried her. She was convinced he would demand more discussion eventually, but at least he hadn't sabotaged her assignment.

The three weeks, all expenses paid, bus tour around Scotland was a very lucky break. The second it had pinged into her email inbox she'd grabbed it. A last minute letdown by the contracted photographer was her gain.

She could telephone conference with her sisters for the business meetings she would miss, and work on Jabbering Gerbera projects on her laptop in the evenings. Apart from the photography and polite socializing with her fellow tour passengers, she would be free to wander through her memories and lick her wounds.

As the bus lurched out of Brick Square toward the motorway, Kitty knew she already missed him. Even packing her bag had been painful. She couldn't wear anything that reminded her of Rosco—her favorite boots now thrown in the back of her walk-in closet. And she'd need to buy a new raincoat at their first scheduled stop.

She propped her weary head against the cold bus window as the gray city views colored her memories. Memories she would never be able to share with anyone else.

The sad, mutual release of confiding their worst childhood traumas. Of understanding each other's pain and abandonment. How she wished she hadn't argued about that. Hadn't spat his support back in his face.

She shivered, remembering their lovemaking warmed by the golden flicker of the fire. Rosco's voice, graveled with passion, calling her "my Kitty" as no one else had ever done.

No. He couldn't have faked *all* of that.

She'd just have to learn to live without him. There was no future for them in fear and innuendo on the social media they both hated.

Tiredness swamped her as she pulled out her cell phone and blocked Rosco's contacts.

Chapter Sixteen

Rosco held his head in his hands, massaged his tired eyes, and forced himself to face his failings.

The townhouse kitchen where Kitty had shared his lamb and potatoes felt empty and bleak. The hard glass table cold and lonely where his housekeeper had laid cutlery for one.

He'd had twenty-four hours of life without Kitty and cursed himself for losing her. For driving her away.

His adult life had been devoted to being as little like his father as possible. Scared to let go, he'd buried his feelings in work and responsibility, and ended up hurting the very people he wanted to protect.

Including himself. And especially Kitty.

He remembered the physical wrench as Kitty flung herself out of the helicopter and stalked away toward the carpark, her heels clicking across the tarmac.

She'd looked so resolute. And he could see the defiant bravery of the ten-year-old girl, hidden away, not wanted in her mother's world.

Hidden away because her mother was ashamed of her, of

the reality of her own life and her daughter's needs.

That was Kitty's life lesson, and it was a knife in his gut to realize he had reinforced it with his business caution and insistence they were safe in their private world.

Somewhere inside her hurt, Kitty thought his care and natural restraint meant he was ashamed of her. Didn't want her in the real world.

He did want her. Only her. The self-reliant, competent woman who had fearlessly argued her case for a contract. Her bravery in entering his house and defying the paparazzi—a complex bravery he now fully understood. Her past was as complicated as his—family hurts that had drawn them to each other.

No, Kitty was wrong. She did family just fine. Just by being herself.

He dragged his fingers through his hair, his memories of the last few days with Kitty filling his senses.

Kitty, pale as they faced the media but savvy enough to lay a false trail. Kitty, eyes shining with mischief under that battered old table, laughing even more as she played goldfish with Cara to make light of their first stolen kiss.

What a kiss. Hot and tempting. Like that damn orange zipper that had been his undoing. Heat slammed through him remembering the unwrapping. The giving and receiving of love that had changed him forever.

He'd never felt this way about a woman, and he knew he never would again. Kitty's heart was safe with him. He may be his father's son, but he would never be his father's man, whatever the media might want to insinuate.

The jumble of thoughts and emotions Kitty had tried to explain suddenly made sense. But she was wrong about one thing.

He *could* sort it.

He could sort the future.

He drew a ragged breath. Kitty was his whole world now, and he intended to prove it. He'd gladly lose face and business to protect their future. To keep her.

He just needed three weeks and three phone calls.

• • •

Three weeks later, Kitty showered off the dust of the bus trip then plastered a smile on her face as she joined her sisters at the Board table. Rosco was never far from her thoughts when she was away, and it was worse now that she was back. Her heart and pride were still bruised, yet the world had, hurtfully, moved on without her.

"I've missed you so much," she said to her sisters. "Thank you for looking after everything without me."

"It was all a pleasure, Kitty. Now we need to get down to business. And more specifically *up* to the rooftop," said Rosa.

"Good thing it isn't raining." Danni gingerly patted her hair, its super-spiky style miraculously elevated by a ton of product. "I'm trialing a new range for my Christmas gift section."

"Very pleased it isn't raining," said Rosa, with a warm smile for Danni. "We'll all need to collect a coat—it will be cool up there—and then meet at the lift."

Kitty shivered, puzzled. "What have I missed?" When she'd gone away their lift access beyond the fourth floor was blocked, as it had been for eighteen months.

"You haven't missed anything, Kitty," said Meg. "In fact you're just in time."

"Rosa's been romancing the bank again." Tessa grinned. "Restoration Stage Two needs some mortgage muscle, and the plans include an enticing rooftop paradise for apartment owners."

"Romancing's the word," agreed Rosa. "The bank isn't as

loving toward our second stage development as it was with the first. We need to present every asset to its full potential to get their financial backing."

Rosa looked at her watch. "Coats," she said. "Ten minutes max. See you all at the lift. Bring your camera, Kitty."

Kitty assessed her wardrobe. All the clothes that screamed Rosco were bundled down on one end, with a hanging divider separating them from anything she hadn't worn with Rosco.

In her coat section, that left her with a choice between an old black anorak and an orange houndstooth fitted dresscoat in fine wool tweed.

Her sad Rosco-deprived heart wanted her to slop around in the anorak feeling sorry for herself.

But her move-on, you're-on-your-own-and-proud survivor spirit slipped into the softly lined tweed and added a chic orange cloche hat.

With her camera around her neck, she joined the others heading for the roof.

The temperature was fresh when they stepped out among the air conditioning units and assorted pipes. "What do you want me to photograph? It needs an awful lot of imagination to see this as exclusive rooftop living."

Rosa checked her watch again. "I want you to photograph the sky." She pointed to a small speck in the distance. "Incoming advertising."

Kitty looked suspiciously at her sisters, who were all wearing big grins, their gazes fixed on the sky. They'd obviously been more busy than she realized while she was away, and they hadn't included her in this decision.

She raised her camera and tracked what she could now see was a helicopter through her viewfinder.

Rosco-radar tingled along her veins as the chopper flew toward them. It was trailing a huge advertising banner.

Her sisters cheered and clapped as the flypast revealed

the banner.

A lump caught in Kitty's throat, and her tears misted the viewfinder.

A ten-meter long goldfish fluttered past her, emblazoned with the words I LOVE YOU, KITTY.

She sobbed as anger, relief, and then melting heat swept over her.

She lowered her camera, too unsteady to focus, as the goldfish swished its feathery tail in the slipstream and fluttered out of the shot.

Her sisters put their arms around her shoulders, holding her upright.

"It's Rosco," said Meg, with a sigh in her voice. "He called us to a meeting as your family and asked for your hand in Rosco-Kittyness." Meg smiled dreamily at the romantic goofiness of it. "Whatever *you* decide that looks like."

He loved her. *Loved* her. And was flying his flag for all the world to see. The implication wasn't lost on her.

"You need to face the sky again," Rosa ordered, placing Kitty in position, helping raise the camera to her face. "He's looping for a second flyby. Don't lose concentration, you'll regret not getting the perfect shot."

Kitty trembled, Rosco-chills chasing the Rosco-heat.

She watched the chopper loom large toward her, clicked her camera twice, then lowered it. Real life demanded she see the big picture.

The goldfish seemed close enough to touch, its huge Gerbera Girl cartoon eye flirting with her. Its tail of feathered fins dancing in the breeze.

The message—I LOVE YOU, KITTY—flashed a neon light in her heart.

Hands circled her waist, holding her fast. A warm Irish burr whispered in her ear. "So would you be considering mutual loving forever, Gerbera Girl? With me, in the real world?"

"Rosco!" She turned in his arms, sobbing and laughing. Her sisters had gone. There was just her and Rosco on the roof. On top of the world.

"Next on my list," she said, smiling through tears she couldn't control. "My Rosco." She touched her hand to his heart. "I love you, too."

"I know you do, Kitty. It shines in your laugh, in your care and passion."

It amazed and humbled her that he'd seen through her hurt and her baggage. "I can't find the words. It's all new to me, this loving."

"Me, too," he murmured, pressing his lips to her cheek with a touch of his Irish mischief. "Cute hat."

"Thanks." She smiled, feeling less teary as her heart hummed to his familiar banter.

• • •

Rosco placed his hand over hers, holding her love to his heart. She loved him and she was smiling again.

He looked down at her, thrilled that his goldfish love note had freed her to be happy. And he loved the way her feelings mirrored his own.

But it wasn't quite enough. They needed to sort through the rubbish as well. Seal it away for good. He needed her to know he would always have her back. He would never let her down as his father had his mother.

"I'm sorry. The tabloid stuff..." His voice broke as he hugged her closer. "I'd give anything to protect you from that."

"I felt so angry and trapped. The bullying, stupidity of it all. For you and me. It burned. Like a fire inside me."

"Aye. You're a hot woman." He smiled, his own eyes as

moist as hers. "That's when I knew I loved you. When you told me you'd still work with me even though I could see you were hurting."

"I was scared, though."

"Me, too. I thought I'd lost you."

"Our true privacy isn't lost. No one shared our under-the-table and Chopper House worlds."

"I think it's safe to assume not even the tabloids could conjure up your under-the-table trick. Only you could make old tablecloths sexy."

That under-the-table sparkle returned to her eyes, tempting him to skip the Trinity St. George saga, but it needed to be finished between them. He stepped back, held her at arm's length, ensuring he could watch her lovely brown eyes grow serious and understand how she had changed his life for the better.

He'd keep it short because he didn't want to pass on the anger and revulsion he'd felt when making the call. "I phoned Trinity St. George. Withdrew from the palace contest."

"No. That was so important to you, to your mother's company." Kitty stiffened in his arms. "My fault."

"Not your fault. My fault for clinging to old wounds. My wounds. My mother wouldn't have tolerated the games. I didn't realize I was playing along. But I was giving them power over my mind when I thought I was in control."

"What did she *say*?" Kitty shook him. "I already know you are above their games."

"She sort of purred, dripping with a love of gossip. Self-righteous hypocrite. She said she was sorry to see me in the scandal media, and I told her I wasn't sorry as it made her intentions clear. I terminated my business with her. Told her I would never consider a contract with her."

"Did she mention me?"

"No." That was true, and he hadn't used Kitty's name once

with that woman. "You were right about her. She's a fake, keeping up her facade to the end. If she'd admitted knowing you she'd be vulnerable to questions about herself."

"That's what I remember from growing up. I expected the same behind your smart London door."

"Well, you were wrong about that." He understood her horror at the paparazzi now. She'd been brought up in all that negative drama, and it wasn't her.

They were empty people, his father and her mother. He hated their cheating, drinking ways. But to allow their influence to reach out and drive him to lock himself away from the risks of love was to deny himself of all that was good.

"You called yourself double trouble, Kitty. But you were wrong about that, too." He watched her eyes cloud then clear as he raised her hand to his lips. "It's your mother and my father who are our double troubles. They owe us our childhoods. But now, together, we owe them—they've shown us what not to be—and they brought us together."

Still holding her hand, he kissed away the tears on her cheeks. Tears of love with the promise of laughter to follow. "We're so alike, Kitty."

"Yes. We were both grounded in hurt. But now," she said, the sparkle he loved returning to her loving brown eyes. "Now, I feel we've set each other free to fly. Like your goldfish banner. Wherever our love takes us."

"Home, soon, would be good. In fact, right now I'll be needing a new home," he said, thumbing her mouth in a lazy circle. "Amanda and Andrew have taken over the townhouse. Could you find me a bed for a while?"

"You can have mine." Her smile against his thumb had his heart kicking with need and love.

"That's a fine offer. Would there be anything I could do to thank you?"

"Unwrap me." She stretched, caught his mouth briefly,

softly, with hers. "Unwrap me on top of our world."

"I'm your man."

He released her coat buttons, burrowed his hands beneath her clothes to claim the warm skin at her waist, and reveled in her answering gasp of pleasure.

"You're even better at this than I remember.

He bent to gently graze her welcoming lips with his. There was no hurry. "We're making new memories now. Golden, lifetime memories."

Acknowledgments

Special thanks to Jo and Gwen for their invaluable friendship and support, and to Wendy Chen, my editor at Entangled Publishing.

About the Author

Suzi Jennings lives in New Zealand and writes international stories of love and laughter. It all started in childhood when she fell in love with reading, scribbled stories about princesses in castles, and grew up to spend way too much money on books.

She writes warm and witty contemporary romances where family secrets, powerful friendships and enduring loves heal hearts and forge happy-ever-afters.

Her characters are feisty, flirty, fun—and talkative! It's a match made in keyboard heaven as Suzi is more than happy to listen. They get their stories told and Suzi gets to enjoy their journeys to each happy ending.

Discover more category romance titles from Entangled Indulgence...

A Millionaire at Midnight

a *Bachelor Auction* novel by Naima Simone

Socialite Morgan Lett is having a run of bad luck. Her fiancé just dumped her, the charity foundation she loves in danger of folding, and the gorgeous man she won at a masquerade bachelor auction turns out to be her cold-hearted new employer. Millionaire Alexander Bishop needs a wife. And Morgan is the perfect candidate. She may drive him crazy, but she needs money to save the foundation she loves, and he needs a fiancée. It's a flawless arrangement—no strings, no love. Until she has him wanting more.

The Billionaire's Runaway Fiancé

an *Invested in Love* novel by Jenna Bayley-Burke

Robyn's new boss has a penchant for running off new personal assistants, but she's not about to let herself be fired by the billionaire with a bad attitude. She's determined to be indispensable and unflappable, until he surprises her with a crazy proposal. Curtis decides his assistant is the answer to his publicity problems if she'll agree to marry him. He can offer her the world—everything he thinks a woman desires. But Robyn wants a happily ever after with a man who loves her. If only he can convince her love is off the table, not to mention convince his heart of that...

The CEO's Seduction

a *Hamilton Family* novel by Diane Alberts

The last thing Brett Ross wants is to be back in the small town he grew up in, but his best friend is getting married, so there's no way he's skipping this visit back home. Anna Hamilton has always been in love with Brett, even if she's always been his best friend's annoying little sister to him. But when he looks at her, she doesn't see annoyance in his eyes anymore. All she needs is to find a way to escape her pesky, protective older brothers… And then the game is *on*.

The Millionaire's Revenge

novel by Wendy Byrne

Luke McCall has a plan to take down the underhanded competitor messing with his livelihood. He intends to romance the man's daughter and get the information he needs to put his rival out of business. He just didn't plan for the way she makes him feel. Grace Wilson has a new philosophy for dealing with men: Test. Screw. Dump. But after she meets Luke, she's not sure she'll be able to walk away. He's sexy and charming and survives every tests she puts him through.

CPSIA information can be obtained
at www.ICGtesting.com
Printed in the USA
LVOW08s1442060317
526286LV00001B/38/P

9 781682 814260